The

MW01601772

Cover Design by Iyiola Olawale
Interior Design by Saige the Gemini
Edited by Rocky Rose

Rose Antrum Empire trade paperback printing
2024

For more information, or to contact the authors,
send an email to:
rockwritepublishing@gmail.com
sthegemini69@gmail.com

Salt & Saige the Gemini

The Initiation Shorts

The Initiation Shorts

Introducing the Anal Assassin & the Anal Princess

"Daron, fuck this pretty ass of mine baby, get deeper baby, ugghhh!"

"You love how I'm fuckin' you, don't you?"

"Damnit baby, you know I do!! FUCK!!"

"Where you want this nut? I'm bout to bust!"

"All over my face baby, you know I love your protein facials."

As I was digging Kyra out, she began throwing her ass back on me, and ass is what she definitely had a lot of, and she knew throwing it back on me was going to make me nut quicker. Just as I was about to nut, I grunted, Kyra got on her knees ready to take all of my man potion onto her face; something about seeing her with my cum all over her face did something to me.

"AHHHH!!" I let out a loud grunt and a large load onto her face, it was the best sight and feeling ever.

"Babygirl, what are your plans for Christmas this year?"

"I'm not sure yet, I know Trice and the girls were thinking about hosting a few holiday themed events at the Palace, I'm sure I'm going to be needed in some form or fashion, why, what's up?"

"I'm thinking about going back home for the week, was wondering if you'd be down to come with me, meet the family and everything."

"Aww boo boo, you ready for me to meet the family?"

"Listen, we've been doing this dance with one another for like what? A year a half? I think it's way past time that you've met my family."

"I'll tell you what, I'll let the girls know that I can help them for a couple of days and I'll make sure I'm in Jersey with you by Christmas Eve, does that work for you?"

"It does my love; are you staying here tonight or going back home?"

"I have to go to the Palace tonight, I can stay here but I won't be back til after I close, is that cool with you?"

"Absolutely, I'm going to come down there about an hour before it's time for you to close so I can walk out with you, I don't want you closing up by yourself and coming back this way that late."

"Another reason why I love you so much, you make sure I'm good at all times."

"You're my baby, I have to make sure you're good, cause if you're not, then I'm not either."

Later that evening

Since Kyra was at the Palace (if you don't know what palace I'm referring to, you should really read The Freak In Me by Saige the Gemini), my brothers and I got together for gentlemen's night, cigars, drinks, spades, and a few strippers.

"D, we appreciate you allowing us to use your rental spot for our gentlemen's night, we definitely needed this tonight," Justice told me.

"No doubt, I know we all have things going on in our lives and I know I for one needed a stress reliever."

"What are y'all doing for the holidays?" JayVon asked the crew.

I responded, "I'm going to Jersey, and I'm going to need your fellas help with something too."

"You know we got you bro, what's goin on?" Levi asked.

"I plan on proposing to Kyra while we're in Jersey, she'll be coming down on Christmas Eve, I want to propose to her on Christmas Day, I'm going to need the ladies help too, but Kyra can't know about it."

"Well damn, congrats bro!! You know whatever you need, we got you. You and Kyra are good together," Justice said.

"I'm probably asking a lot but I would love it if everyone could be there and hopefully some of the ladies can contact her family and have them come up to be able to witness it."

"Trice and I can definitely help with that, I'll change our flights, we're going to Atlanta to spend Christmas with her grandparents and her aunt and uncle."

"That's what's up, I appreciate you bro, but I don't want you to have to change your plans on account of me."

"It's not a problem bro, we were leaving out of New York anyway, leaving out of Jersey isn't much of a change, told you we got you."

"Justice, I know you and Akira are kind of still on the outs with one another, but do you

think you can pass the news along? I

know Kyra would love to have her there."
"I got you, I gotta go talk to her anyway, this shit between us has been going on long enough and I don't want to keep stressing her, especially since she's pregnant."

"Do you think y'all can work through this?" JayVon asked his brother."
"I'm hoping we can, I can't and won't lie to y'all, I miss my wife and I miss seeing my son

everyday, tucking him into bed, waking up to him in the morning jumping in our bed."

"Go make it right bro, you already know that back in college you and Akira were relationship goals for Trice and I, the both of you have too much skin in the game to let some shit like this break y'all up."

"I know, I'm going to make it right with her soon, I just gotta get my head right. Daron, Akira and I will be there to support you and Kyra, you got my word on that."

"I appreciate that bro, Kyra having her sorority sisters there to share the moment with her is going to be major."

"Are you nervous?" Levi asked.
"Nervous is an understatement, I've been shittin' bricks ever since I bought the ring."

"Everything is going to work out, the both of y'all are a match perfectly made, both freaks," Levi said laughing.

"Man, what you mean? All of us got a bunch of freaks in our women, you do realize that Delta Pi Psi is just the female version of Beta Delta Mu, right? I swear the founders for both of the organizations must've had a meeting of the minds and came up with this shit together, two organizations whose primary initiation process is focused around sex, fucking genius!!"

"Yea, I would have loved to have been in the meeting of the minds when the brothas came up with the concept. Y'all know Trice's whole family is BDM and DPP, right? Like her parents, aunt, uncle and grandparents," JayVon responded.

"Speaking of Trice, when are you two getting married? Y'all already got the family dynamic and her family loves the hell out of you, when you plan on poppin' the question?" I asked him.

"This weekend while we're in Atlanta with her family, her aunt, uncle and sister have been helping me plan everything, I figured there'd be no better time than while the whole family will be together."

All of us congratulated JayVon on his pending engagement, our ladies were going to be pleasantly surprised this weekend, two sorority sisters getting engaged days apart from one another, it was going to be epic.

As the night continued the guys and I smoked cigars, had a few drinks, enjoyed the strippers from the DyNasty Playland, and played cards. Around twelve in the morning I told the guys I had to bounce so I could meet Kyra at the club so she wouldn't have to walk out alone.

"Aight fellas, I'm bout to bounce, y'all can stay as long as you'd like but I have to meet Kyra at the club since she's closing tonight, I don't want her walking out by herself."

"You know the girls have security with them until they close, right?" Julius asked.

"I know, but I told Kyra I'd be there before they close to walk out with her, security is cool but I need to make sure my woman is safe and secure."

"You gonna have the other girls wanting us to do that shit now, just watch, when it's Marie's night to close, she's going to be expecting me to come to the club and wait for her."

"Is that such a bad thing? Your woman's safety should be your first priority, I don't even go to bed until Kyra tells me she's home safe and sound."

"It's a bad thing if I'm out and doing other shit, or if I already have my evening planned before she mentions to me that she wants me there when she closes," Julius replied.

"I don't even know why I asked you that shit, you wouldn't even walk your shorties out when we were in college. It could be late as hell and you'd kick them out of the room without even making sure they got to their cars or dorms safely, some shit just never changes, does it?"

"Whatever bro," he replied, obviously irritated.

"Is there trouble in paradise with you and Marie?" Justice asked.

"Trouble ain't the word bro, I'm bout ready to break it off from her and move back to Philly, I think she's starting to get the marriage bug and I'm not on that type of time."

"Y'all have been going hard with each other for over five years now, you know women be on their biological clocks, ready to settle down and start a family, if you think it's not something you want with her, y'all need to talk so she can be with someone who wants the same things as she does, but before you have that talk, you need to make sure you can stomach her being with someone else, doing everything she does to you or even more," Justice told him.

"Why the fuck would I want to imagine something like that?"

"I know Marie, she's a damn good woman and the minute you tell her that you no longer want to be with her, there are going to be a million men waiting to get with her, so make sure you can handle seeing her at the business functions with her new dude, and going home with him and doing all the freaky shit she used to do with you; just be prepared," JayVon chimed in.

Julius sat in silence for about five minutes then said, "I got some heavy thinking to do, once the new year comes in, I'll know what I want to do."

"Ain't none of us getting any younger bro, just think about that, and Marie has stuck by your side even with all of the fucked up *things you've done to her over the years, take that shit into consideration too, so think long and hard before you cut it off with the only woman who has held you down all these years, cause when she's gone, she'll be gone forever," I added before leaving to meet Kyra.*

"I'll see y'all later, I'm out, Justice, you have the spare key, right? You can lock up after y'all are done, I'm staying at Kyra's tonight."

"Bet, yo, have you heard from Dre? He hasn't been responding to any of the group messages, hasn't been answering any of my phone calls or anything," Justice asked.

"Yea, I talked to him not too long ago, he and Jade split like a month ago and he hasn't been taking it too well."

"Damn, ain't even know, well if he hits you soon, tell him to hit my line," Justice said.

"Will do, I will see you good brothas in Jersey later this week."

"Aight bro, see you soon," the brothers responded to me before I left.

As I was getting in my car, I sent Kyra a message to let her know that I was on my way."

"*Hey beautiful, just letting you know that I'm on my way to the club now, I will see you in about ten minutes.*"

She promptly responded, "*Hey baby, I was beginning to think you forgot about me since I hadn't heard from you. I have a surprise for you when you get here, I won't be at the DyNasty Pleasure Palace, so come on up to the DyNasty Playground when you get here.*"

"What is she up to tonight?" I asked myself aloud. Kyra always kept me on my toes and was always doing some spontaneous shit, which is another reason I love her so much.

When I got to the Palace, I took the elevator up to the DyNasty Playground and as soon as I got off the elevator I heard "Seems

Like You're Ready" playing through the sound system, "What the hell is goin' on in there?"

As soon as I opened the door to the Playground, I saw Kyra standing on the main stage wearing her sorority colors negligee and heels.

"Well, hello handsome, I'm glad you could finally make it, take a seat, sit back and enjoy the show; tips are welcomed but not mandatory."

"I'm definitely going to enjoy the show, can a brotha possibly get a private dance afterwards?"

"Anything you want, I got you baby," she said as she began moving her body to the beat of the music.

Kyra's moves on the stripper pole were nothing short of amazing, she had moves that I'd never seen before, but it also explained why she was so flexible in bed.

The way she sauntered over to me from the stage had my dick standing at attention, she was definitely about to get the business right here in the middle of the DyNasty Playground.

Kyra began grinding on me, she placed my hands on both of her breasts as she slowly danced on me, I swear she was the best and sexiest non-stripper, stripper I've ever laid my eyes on.

"Are you enjoying your private show?"
"You damn real I am. You don't feel how hard you got my dick?"

"Oh, I most definitely feel it baby, and I'm going to take care of him in just a moment, we just have to go back to the VIP room I have set up for us."

"We don't need the VIP room love, we can get it poppin right here."
"I have a surprise set up for you in the VIP room, it's something you've always wanted, now

follow me please," she told me as she grabbed my hand and led the way.

When we got to the VIP room, there were at least three cameras set up in different parts of the room, my dick got harder just thinking about making love to my love and being able to film it so we could watch it whenever we wanted.

Kyra kissed me slowly and passionately as she began to undress me, she planted small sensual kisses on my neck, then all over my chest until she got to my already rock hard dick.

She sat me down on the couch, pressed the record button on the remote control and the red lights all three cameras popped on, it was definitely showtime. Kyra took my rock hard penis into her warm mouth, and she began sucking it so slow, savoring every minute of it. I loved how she sucked my dick with no hands, she always made it a priority to make me feel good and relax me. As she was sucking the soul out of me I began finger fucking her pussy and ass at the same time. The moans coming from her were letting me know that she was in pure bliss, but I wasn't sure if it was because I was finger fucking her or because she was sucking my dick, Kyra had a thing for getting hella pleasure out of pleasing me.

"Come bounce that ass on this dick baby," I told her.

"Nope, you know how I want it, daddy, my ass has been craving you since I left you earlier today."

"You know I'm going to take care of that ass, but he needs to be wrapped up in that tight ass pussy first, you know daddy is going to take care of all of your holes baby, I got you."

Before I entered her tight, wet pussy, I had to eat her out. The way she blessed my dick, it was only right that I returned the favor.

"Baby, you know you're about to make me orgasm from eating my pussy, your tongue is lethal," she told me while cupping both of her breasts.

"I know, but you also know it's my duty to keep and leave you satisfied, in every area of life, now shut up and let me eat my dinner."

I ate her pussy like I was starving and she was the last meal on earth, orgasm after orgasm ripped through her body for the betterment of twenty minutes. I slid my rock hard dick into her throbbing wet pussy, and I ain't gon' lie, I had to pause for a little while cause if I moved, I was going to burst prematurely.

I began slowly stroking Kyra's pussy and I could feel her tightening her walls around me, I began to rub her clit, and another explosive orgasm ripped through her body. "Baby, you ain't playin' fair! The things you do to my body should be illegal," she said out of breath.

"I've only just begun my love, now tell daddy how much you love this dick."

"Baby, you're the best I've ever had. Your dick is so big, baby, you're gonna stretch me out!"

"Is it too much for you? Do you want me to pull out?"

"Please don't! I can handle it, but you know where I want you to fuck me at, I need all of that dick in my pretty tight ass baby."

I gave her another five or six strokes before I pulled out and gently entered her tight ass, quiet as it's kept, I think Kyra preferred anal sex over vaginal any day and I wasn't one to complain, she had the right one in me cause they don't call me the Anal Assassin for nothing.

I wasn't even in her ass a good five minutes before her body began trembling because of another orgasm. After an hour and a half of pleasure we both climaxed together, we were both so spent, we didn't feel like moving a muscle, but we both got dressed, cut the video cameras, made sure we got the tapes out of them, locked up all the businesses and locked the main door.

I felt bad cause Kyra's security guard had to wait til she was out the building before he could leave and it was definitely my fault that she took so long locking up after the DyNasty Pleasure Palace and the DyNasty Playground closed for the evening. Her security guard pulled off first, then Kyra pulled off and I pulled off last just to make sure I had eyes on her and her vehicle at all times.

We pulled up to her house about twenty minutes later and her security guard waved as he made sure Kyra was good and made his way to his next destination. As soon as we got into her house, we both went to the master bathroom and showered together.

"Babe, how long should I plan on being in Jersey for the holiday, need to figure out what to pack?"

"I'm going to say about two or three days, I was going to ask you if you wanted to go to Atlanta afterwards for a few days, just to chill for a little."

"That'll be a nice little getaway, I think Trice is going down there for the holiday too, so hopefully her, Jay, you and myself can hang a little while we're down there."

"That'll be dope, I think Justice and JayVon still have their house down there, so I can see if it'll be okay for us to stay there while we're down there."

"It would be dope if Trice and JayVon stayed there as well, we can spend some time with one another."

"Have you spoken to Jade lately?"
"I talk to my sister everyday, why, what's up?"

"Nothing, the fellas were asking me earlier if I had heard from Dre lately, they said they'd been trying to call and text him but he hasn't responded to any of their messages. I don't think he's taking the breakup well."

"Damn, that sucks, but he has no one to blame but himself. He did my girl dirty and when she got her lick back, he couldn't handle it, fuckin' idiot."

"I don't think he's an idiot bae, but you're right that he only has himself to blame, sometimes I think being in an erotic fraternity comes with a certain reputation that some people feel as if they have to live up to, and Dre got caught up and caught out."

"Listen, as long as you know the grass ain't greener on the other side, we shouldn't have anything to worry about."

"Kyra, you know you're the only woman for me, I don't want anyone else, I love you and only you."

"What's love got to do with anything? Dre claimed he loved Jade and look at how he did her."

"Love is an action, not just a feeling, and I feel as if I do a pretty damn good job at showing and telling you that I love you and am in love with you, do you not agree?"

"I do agree. Can I ask you something?"

"Shoot."

"Do you see us having a future together?"

"I absolutely do, I just told you that you're the only woman for me and that I don't want anyone else."

"I know, but you and I both know that feelings can change in the blink of an eye, and I don't want either one of us to be madly in love with one another one minute and the next we're going our separate ways because that love has faded away."

"Baby girl, you are my heart, the only thing that could make me not want to be with you anymore is if you stepped out on me or did some fucked up shit to me, other than that, nothing you can say or do that would make me not want to be with you."

Christmas Eve

My family and I rented an event space to have Christmas dinner because my family was too big to host it at anyone's house in Jersey. We had a DJ, photographer, lots of food, fun laughter and a damn good time. After everyone finished eating, I figured it would be the perfect time to surprise Kyra. Justice and Akira, JayVon and Trice, Levi and Kiera were all there to support Kyra and I in what I hoped to be one of the happiest days of our lives; I was even able to have her parents fly in, I couldn't do this properly without those who she loved the most there to witness it.

The DJ began playing Eric Benét's Spend My Life With You ever so softly, the lights began to dim, the ambiance was perfect. I grabbed the mic from the DJ and asked Kyra to come stand by me. By her facial expression, I could see she was nervous and trying to figure out what the hell was going on.

"Daron, what is happening?"

"Look into the crowd baby, do you see anyone you recognize?"

She began looking around at all of the people that were sitting and standing, and then the waterworks began when she spotted her parents. She looked at her parents then said, "Y'all told me you were going on a cruise for the holiday!" Everyone laughed.

"Kyra Denise Jordan, I love you with all my heart, you make my days longer and my nights brighter, you make my heart smile from the inside out, and I don't want to spend my life with anyone else. Everything we've built over the past few years have been amazing, but now, I want to build a family and an even larger empire. Kyra, would you do me the honor of being my wife?"

The tears began again, her whole body trembling with excitement, then she said barely above a whisper, "Hell yes I'll be your wife!"

Everyone in the room began clapping and her line sisters were the first to run up to her to congratulate her on her engagement.

"Oh my God Kyra!! Congratulations girl!" Trice said, wiping tears from her own eyes. "Y'all knew about this, didn't you?"

"You know we did, you know the men wouldn't have been able to pull all of this off by themselves," Marie said laughing and wiping tears from her eyes.

"Marie, I didn't see Julius, he didn't come with you?" Kyra asked.
"Hell no, quiet as it's kept, I'm not sure him and I are going to be rockin' with each other too much longer, the vibe between us has been off for some time now, and I'm at my wits end trying to figure out what the hell is wrong with him or where this relationship is going."

"I hate to hear that, a few years ago, we all had our men and everything was great, now look at us, some of us are still with our men, Jade and Dre have called it quits, this shit is sad," Kyra said shaking her head.

"Enough about everyone else, let us get a look at this ring!" Akira said.

As the women and Kyra's family were talking, my parents, my frat brothers and childhood friends went outside to have a few celebratory cigars.

"So Jay, are you nervous about tomorrow?" I asked him.

"Nah, not really, I mean, we already have our family with the babies, I just want to make an honest woman out of her before we have more children."

"More, you got your boy and girl already, and you trying to have more? Does Trice know about you wanting more children?"

"Yea, we've discussed it, she's ready, you know the ladies' businesses are booming, so it's kinda like the best time to do it. Justice, you and Akira coming tomorrow?"

"Last I checked we were flying down with y'all, that's what Akira told me, she handled all of the flight details, I was just told to show up."

All of us laughed, it was good to see that Akira and Justice seemed to be working things out. "Kyra and I will be leaving in the morning, so we'll be down there for your big moment, just text me the details and we'll be there.

"The whole family will be at our old crib, so you already know if y'all need a place to stay, there's more than enough room at the crib."

"Bet, we're going to take you up on that, Kyra and I were just talking about that a few days ago."

"Mr. Hughes, how do you feel about your son and Kyra being engaged now?" Levi asked my pops.

"Kyra is a good woman, she keeps my son on the straight and narrow, he'd be a damn fool to let her go, I'm happy I'm getting another daughter soon."

"Yea, Kyra is top notch, and she's definitely the one to keep your head on your shoulders," Justice told me.

"Yo, shut up bruh!" I replied laughing. "Listen I'm 'bout to be out, our flight leaves in about two hours and I'm pretty sure Trice still has some packing to do," JayVon told me.

Justice then said, "I guess I need to be heading out too, we will see y'all tomorrow, hit us when you get close to the crib so we can make sure one of us is home."

"Bet, I'll see y'all tomorrow, Kyra and I have some private celebrating to do later tonight before we hop on the plane tomorrow."

"If y'all are real freaks you'll get your mile high membership tomorrow," Levi said to me.

"Oh, that's definitely going to happen but we'd have to be on a night flight, I heard it's best to do it at night."

"Time for me to leave, I see where this conversation is headed," my pops said to us before going back inside.

"My bad pops, almost forgot you were out here with us!" Levi responded, dapping my father up.

We all put our cigars out and went back inside to join the rest of the party. As soon as I walked back in, Krya ran to me and jumped into my arms.

"You have made me the happiest woman in the world today, you know that, right?"

"Hmm, is that right? How did I ever manage to do that?"

"Baby, you flew my parents in, my line sisters are here and even some of my friends from back home, and you put this damn rock on my finger, I love you so much."

"I love you more and I knew that you would want your family and friends here to celebrate this special occasion with you, you deserve all of this and more."

"I don't know if I've ever told you how much I appreciate you, but I do and I value you and our relationship. I thank you for who you are to me."

"You don't have to thank me for that Kyra, you are my rib, it's my job and my pleasure to hold you down in any and every capacity you need."

"Can we ditch this party and go get busy now? I know we have an early flight in the morning."

"Your wish is my command."

We said our goodbyes to our family and friends, told them we had to go pack for our trip to

Atlanta in the morning, and that we'd be in contact with them regarding the wedding plans.

When we got to our hotel we were all over each other, Kyra basically had my hard dick halfway out of my pants by the time we got to the elevator, so we were already very hot and bothered. When we made it to our room, our clothes were practically off, I picked Kyra up, and ate her pussy standing up, orgasm after orgasm ripped through her body and I had no plans of letting up off her anytime soon. With every orgasm I gave her my dick seemed to have gotten harder, and it brought me pleasure knowing that I was bringing her mounds and mounds of pleasure.

I laid her down on the bed and took a minute to take in her beauty. This woman was about to be my wife, and I was excited to be able to please her for the rest of our lives.

"Are you going to just stare at me or are you going to give me that dick?"

"I'm going to do both since you asked," I responded while taking my time and becoming one with my future wife.

As soon as I entered her, she gasped, then another orgasm ripped through her body, more powerful than the ones she had when I was eating her out standing up. We made slow, passionate love, something we hadn't done in a long while. There was something about looking into each other's eyes, holding hands, and just enjoying one another that hit on a whole different level.

Christmas Day

"Babe, our flight leaves in about two hours, we need to get to the airport within the next fifteen minutes, are you all packed and ready?"

"I am all ready to go, I packed earlier this morning, I even packed your bags for you."

"You are really the best, I don't know what I'd do without you."

"I don't know what I'd do without you either. Being as though we have to leave like now, that means we won't be able to stop by your parents to see them today, that kinda sucks."

"They aren't home, they're on their way to Dubai for a few weeks, they left shortly after the party last night."

"Well damn, I'm trying to be like them when I grow up, going out of the country for a few weeks with not a care in the world."

"Bae, you know damn well if we wanted to do that now, we could, our businesses are booming, we've both hit millionaire status, on our way to multimillionaire status, all you gotta do is say the word and we can book our flights and be gone for a few weeks to wherever you want to go."

"How would you feel about a destination wedding?"

"I'm with it if that's what you want to do, as long as you're happy, then I'm happy my love."

"I think it'll be dope and I think it'll be a good time with your LB's and my LS's, especially the ones that are going through it right now. I'm hoping our wedding and our love will be able to give them a renewed look at love, especially with Jade and Dre."

"Shit, Marie and Julius might need it too, the way he was talking the other night, he's not sure he sees a future with Marie."

"If that's the case then he needs to let her go so she can get wifed up by a man who loves her for her and who can handle her in every aspect of her life. If Julius feels like he's not that man, he needs to hit the bricks and make a clean break."

"Damn ma, tell me how you really feel."

"I'm just tired of men being in these long term relationships then when the woman is ready to settle down, make the relationship official, get married, have children, men begin to act their dick size instead of being real men and handling responsibility, shit irritates me to no end!"

"Listen, I wholeheartedly agree, now let's go so we can catch this flight and make it to Atlanta to celebrate this holiday, our car service is waiting for us."

In Atlanta

We finally made it to Atlanta, grabbed our rental then called Justice to see if they were at the crib so we could get settled in.

"Bro bro, what's good brotha? Just calling to see if you or your brother are at the crib, Kyra and I are headed your way now."

"What's good brotha? We are actually at Trice's aunt and uncle's house, I'll shoot you the address so you can make your way over here."

"We don't want to impose, we can go sightseeing or grab something to eat until y'all get back to the crib."

"Nonsense, Aunt Chele and Uncle Brian are excited to meet the both of you, so bring your asses on over here, I just sent you the address."

"Bet, we will see y'all in a little while."
"So, apparently, everyone is at Trice's aunt and uncle's house, so we're going to head over there."

"That's fine, I hope they have food cooked, I'm starving."
"So am I, that's why I told Justice we could go grab something to eat or go sightseeing while they were over there but he insisted that we go; these are southern folk, I'm sure they have food prepared."

We made it to where the crew was and Trice and JayVon greeted us at the door before we had a chance to ring the doorbell.

"There's the newly engaged couple!" Trice said with probably too much excitement.

"Sistaaa!" Kyra greeted her as if she didn't just see her last night.

"I'm glad y'all could make it, I'm surprised y'all decided to come to the A, especially after your engagement party last night."

"We knew mostly everyone would be down here for the holidays, plus you know Atlanta is our old stomping grounds, so it's mostly a nostalgic moment, the brothas back together again," I told Trice.

"Speaking of the engagement party, I know you knew about it and you didn't even give me a hint as to what was about to happen!" Kyra said to Trice.

"I was not about to ruin the surprise for you and have Jay and Daron mad at me, hell no," Trice replied.

"I wouldn't have been mad at you, love, I just would not have told you another secret for a long time," JayVon replied.

"*I second JayVon's emotions,*" *I said to Trice.*

"*Listen, I don't mean to be rude, but does your aunt have anything to eat? We are both starving. We didn't have time to eat before we left the hotel this morning, and the last time either of us had anything to eat was last night at the party,*" *Kyra asked Trice and JayVon.*

"*Well, that's not totally true, I did eat after the party, but it was definitely a different type of food,*" *I said to Kyra laughing.*

"*TMI bro, tmi, but yes, my aunt and uncle have a full spread laid out in the house, so let's go!*"

As soon as we walked into the house, the heavenly aroma of sweet potato pie, apple pie, baked macaroni and cheese, spiral ham, fresh collard greens smacked us right in the face.

"*Auntie Chele, Uncle Brian, these are our friends, Daron and Kyra, who are also members of Beta Delta Mu and Delta Pi Psi. Daron and*

Kyra, these are the two responsible for raising me and making me the woman I am today, my Aunt Chele and Uncle Brian."

"It's a pleasure to meet the both of you, we've heard so many great things about you from Trice and Jay," Kyra said, extending her hand to Ms. Chele.

"Put that hand away, we hug over here," Ms. Chele said, hugging Kyra.

Mr. Brian and I dapped it up and Ms. Chele and I embraced in a hug.

"I'm sure the both of you are hungry, there's a bathroom down the hall to the left that you can use to wash your hands, then you can fix yourselves a plate, we've been waiting for you to get here before we ate."

"I truly hope we're not imposing, I told Justice that we could go sightseeing or something so y'all could spend time together," I said to Ms. Chele.

"Nonsense, any friends of Trice and JayVon are family to us, and now that we're about to break bread together, you're definitely family," Uncle Brian replied.

Kyra and I both went to the bathroom to freshen up a bit and get ready to break bread with Trice's family.

"So Kyra, have you begun planning your wedding?" Ms. Chele asked.

"Not yet, but Daron and I did discuss this morning about having a destination wedding, so we just have to choose a destination and plan something small and intimate."

"That's going to be nice, no sense in circulating a lot of money on a wedding when that money can go towards a better investment," Ms. Chele said.

"So Daron, Justice and JayVon tell us that you went to school down here with them, have you ever thought about moving back down here?"

"I have put much thought into it, I'm just trying to convince Kyra that our businesses will be more lucrative in the south."

"Listen, with the gold mine all of y'all have, it's going to flourish anywhere you set up shop, and you know, the homes are less expensive down here and you get more home for your money," Mr. Brian said.

"Exactly Mr. Brian."

"None of that Mr. Brian stuff, you can call me Unc and you can call my wife Auntie, but please no Mister or Missus."

"Bet Unc."

"Jay, where is Justice?"

"He and Akira had to run out for a little while, they should be back soon though."

"Oh, aight, bet."

For the next hour and a half we all sat around Auntie Chele and Uncle Brian's table, talked about business, college life, and everything in between. Kyra and Trice went off with Aunt Chele so Uncle Brian, JayVon and myself went to the back porch to have a few cigars and talk amongst ourselves.

"So nephew, are you all set for tomorrow?" Uncle Brian asked JayVon in a low tone.

"As ready as I'll ever be Unc, just a little nervous and I'm not sure why."

"You're nervous because it's a different level of responsibility. I'm glad you're making an honest woman out of my niece."

"That was a must Unc, you know I love that woman way too much to not make it right, plus we already have our little family, I'd be a fool not to wife her."

"So, for tomorrow, Chele and I are going to come get Trice in the morning so y'all can decorate and get everything together, correct?"

"Yes, sir."

"Good enough."

The Next Day

Auntie Chele and Uncle Brian came through to the crib around ten in the morning to get Trice and Kyra so the rest of the ladies and us men could decorate the house, get the food together and get prepared for the best surprise of Trice's life.

Trice and JayVon definitely deserved all the happiness that was coming to them in the next chapter of their lives. By five in the evening the house had been completely transformed, Trice's grandparents, mother, children, and the rest of her line sister's had flown in, as well as JayVon's family from Connecticut. Uncle Brian and Auntie Chele had sent a text to me asking if it was clear to bring Trice back to the house, and I replied it was time.

Kyra had a blindfold prepped for Trice for when they were a block away from the house so she wouldn't be able to see all the cars that were lined up and down the street. When they were two minutes out Kyra sent me a text telling me to get everyone ready.

JayVon had tealight candles lit in the shape of a heart, her sorority colors rose petals all over the floor, he was donned in a three-piece suit, fresh haircut, looking like he had just stepped out of the GQ magazine.

Brian McKnight's "More Than Wonderful" began playing softly through the speakers, JayVon met Trice and Kyra at the door, he took Trice by the hand and led her to the middle of the living room, then slid her blindfold off.

"Baby, what the hell is going on here?" Trice asked as she began surveying the room and laying eyes on all of the people who mattered the most to her.

"This is the beginning of the rest of our lives together. Trice Pennington, the day we met was definitely under unusual circumstances, but that day was the day that I knew you'd ultimately be my wife. You have come into my life and have made me so much happier. You came in and filled a void that I'd been missing and yearning for even before I knew I was missing it. You are my best friend, my homie, and my forever lover, will you do me the honor of being my wife?"

Tears streamed down her face, she wasn't even able to articulate words, all she could do was shake her head in the affirmative.

"I'm assuming that's a yes?"
"Hell yes I'll be your wife, I've told you a thousand times that you're stuck with me and that you're never getting rid of me!"

JayVon slid the ring on her left ring finger and then kissed her like he'd been missing her for days.

Trice's mother, sister and grandparents all surrounded her, taking turns congratulating her and looking at her ring.

"Two Delta Pi Psi engagements in one week, these DPP weddings are about to be something serious!" Trice's sister, Laniyah said.

"Trice, what do you think about a double destination wedding?" Kyra asked her.

"I think it would be dope, no sense in having our sorority sisters paying for two different weddings, we can do one destination, two weddings and be done with it."

"Do y'all think the men would go for it?" "Are they going to have a choice?" Trice said laughing.

Laniyah then said, "Listen, after the holidays, y'all should all come to New York to our mother's house and we can all help plan the weddings."

"That's a great idea sis, you know mommy, auntie Chele and Big Mama are going to take over the planning. Kyra, do you think your mother will have an issue coming to New York to help us plan?"

"Not at all, even if I have to drive to Philly to pick her up and bring her there, she'll be there."

"Bet, it's a date then."

Once all of the guests left for the evening, Justice, JayVon, Julius, Levi and I along with our ladies all decided to pour up the drinks and just have a great ass time together.

"Ayo Justice, remember that time we had those initiation tricks over here?" Levi asked.

"Hell yea, those were the damn days."

"Man, I kind of miss our college days, carefree, and hella fun."

"Wait, what initiation tricks y'all have over here?" Akira asked with her eyebrows raised.

"The big brothers had specific girls come over here as one of our initiation tasks. I haven't seen any of them since that night, so you have nothing to worry about Akira."

"Never said I was worried, but I damn sure don't remember you mentioning them to me at any time."

"It wasn't anything to tell, but since we're on the subject, did you tell me about your initiation tasks that you had to do? Did you tell me about you having to suck one of my big brother's dicks during your private initiation session?

"WHOA!!! Timeout y'all, this is some shit y'all need to handle in private, not in front of everyone," Levi interjected.

"I'm over this shit, I'm going back home tonight. Trice and Kyra, congratulations on your engagements, I will see and talk to you ladies after the holidays. To my brothers, I love y'all and I hope to see y'all after the holidays too," Akira said, grabbing her bag and heading towards the door.

I felt bad for Akira and Justice, but now that they began to air everything out, I understand a little more now why Justice had been keeping his distance.

After Justice ran after Akira, the air in the house seemed a bit lighter. The drinks were still flowing and we were all feeling right. I happened to glance over to my left and there were Trice and JayVon, naked as the day they were born on the couch intertwined in the 69 position, moans and groans coming from the both of them.

Seeing them made Kyra and I feel some type of way, so Kyra came and sat on my face as I ate her pretty pussy. Julius and Marie and Levi and Kiera even got in on the action, and the next thing I knew, we were all in our own little world having a big ass orgy in the middle of the room, and no one was complaining.

A Year Later...

Sans Souci Resort, Ochos Rios, Jamaica
"Baby, this resort is absolutely stunning!!" Kyra squealed to me.

"This is a dope spot love, you and Trice did the damn thing in planning this double wedding. You know they have a private nude beach and pool, right?"

"Of course I know, that's one of the things that sold Trice and I on this specific resort."

"Do you know if the rest of the crew made it in yet?"

"I think Trice and JayVon should be arriving within the next ten minutes, Justice and Akira are coming in tomorrow with Levi and Kiera. Marie and Jade are coming in later this afternoon. I'm not sure about Dre and Julius, those are your boys since they broke things off with my girls."

"Kyra, please be nice to them this weekend, let us just get through the wedding and afterwards you'll have limited interaction with them."

"I'm good love, the girls and I are going to do our thing, you and the guys can do your own thing, then in two days, I will become Mrs. Hughes, and everyone will be happy."

"Anything you say baby, are you hungry? We can go check out one of the restaurants and find something that suits us."

"Sounds like a plan to me."

We both showered quickly, got dressed and headed to check out the restaurants on the resort. We went to the bar first, I ordered a rum and coke and Kyra ordered an orange cranberry vodka cocktail. Just as we were being seated, Trice and JayVon were walking into the same restaurant.

"Well well, if it isn't the blushing bride!" Kyra said, greeting Trice with a hug.

"Hey soror!! This resort is breathtaking! I think we should have our fifth chapterversary here."

"That would be incredible."

"JayVon, what's good bro?" I asked dapping him up.

"Nothing much good brotha, are you all ready for the ceremony?"

"As ready as I'll ever be, how bout you?"

"Hell yea, I can't wait to be this woman's husband."

"That's what's up, y'all wanna sit together to eat? Justice asked us.

"Sure," I told him.

The waitress sat us at a table with the best view of the island, then Kyra said, "This resort is everything, we did the damn thing Trice."

Trice replied, "We sure did. When are your parents coming in?"

"They should be in tonight, what about your family?"

"Everyone should be in tonight, Laniyah and my mother are traveling with the twins and Big Mama, Pops Auntie Chele and Uncle Brian are traveling together."

"I can't wait to see my niece and nephew, I know they're getting big. When we get back and settled, Daron and I are going to have to get them for a weekend."

"Just let us know when and they will be packed and ready for y'all."

"Daron, you want children?" Justice asked me.

"Hell yea, can't wait to knock this woman up!!"

"JayVon, please don't get this man started, ever since you and Trice announced y'all were pregnant he's been on me about having children."

JayVon began laughing then said, "My bad sis, but I know y'all are going to make great parents."

For the betterment of the next hour or so the four of us sat, ate and talked about the itinerary leading up to the wedding. I couldn't believe in 48 hours I'd be marrying the woman of my dreams, and having a double wedding with one of my line brothers.

2 days later...Day of the Wedding...

"Trice, I tried my dress on a week before coming out here and it was perfect, now it's not fitting and I promise you I've been watching what I eat so I made sure I didn't gain any weight just for this wedding."

"Kyra, when was your last period?"
"I'm not pregnant, I think it's stress weight, is that a thing?"

"I'm sure it can be but I'm almost positive you're pregnant. Think about it, you started throwing up after we left dinner a couple of days ago, you were irritable, snappy and uninterested in the bachelorette party last night, check your app, and see how long ago it's been since you had your last period."

Kyra grabbed her phone, opened the health app on her phone and almost immediately threw her phone across the room. "Fuck! She yelled out."

Kiera, Marie, Jade and Akira came running into the room to see what was happening.

Kiera asked, "Kyra, you alright sis?"
"Hell no I'm not alright, I think I'm pregnant y'all."

"Aww sis!! Congratulations!!" Jade said, hugging her.
"Ain't this some shit!! I can't even drink and celebrate my damn wedding like I want tonight, this shit is for the birds!" Kyra said as she began to cry.

"K, don't cry, you're going to mess up your makeup, this is supposed to be the happiest day of your life. I'll contact the team downstairs and tell them to make sure you have mocktails for tonight, you can still celebrate tonight without the alcohol, besides, you don't want to be drunk celebrating your wedding night, you want to be able to remember the night," Akira told her.

"I know, I'm just irritated, my fuckin' dress ain't even fitting right."

"Luckily for you, I'm great with a needle and thread, I'll take it out a little in the midsection and you won't even know the difference by the time I'm done. How much time do we have before I have to head to the beach?" Marie said.

"We need to be leaving within the next ten minutes," Trice responded.
"Bet, more than enough time."

Marie helped Kyra with her dress, Jade fixed up Kyra's makeup and hair and Akira helped Trice put the finishing touches on her final look. The photographer we hired came in and started taking candid photos of the ladies.

Gentlemen's suite..

"Let's all raise our glasses to our line brothers, friends, and sons, Daron and JayVon as they get ready to embark on the next chapter of life, fellas, I for one am proud of the both of you, making honest women out of your ladies, I know my sisters are proud to be your women and I know with Kyra and Trice in your corners, they best is yet to come of the both of you, salute to you kings!" Levi said.

"Thanks bro, I appreciate it," I responded. Then Justice said, "Thanks fam, I appreciate it too. I think I speak for Daron, Kyra, Trice and myself when I say thank you to all of you for being able to make it to our wedding, we know the holiday season can be a bit overwhelming, but to have y'all away from family during the holidays, we take none of this for granted, so thank you and cheers to yourselves."

"Y'all ready to be the next two married men of the crew?" Justice asked both JayVon and I.

"I know I am, you know how I feel about Kyra, shit, you and Akira are the ones who introduced us to one another, and I'm not sure I ever thanked y'all for that, but that was the greatest thing the two of you could've done for me," I told Justice.

"No doubt bro, you know I wouldn't even introduce you to someone unless I felt that she'd be good for you. I'm just glad the both of you hit it off the way you did."

"Listen fellas, I hate to break up this bromance, but we need to get down to the beach within the next three minutes so we're not late and so the ladies don't cuss us out," Julius said to us.

The Ceremony

Monica's "Everything to Me" began playing as Kyra and Trice made their way down the aisle, and I'm not going to lie, there wasn't a dry eye out there, including mine. Kyra had this glow about her as she was walking down the aisle, she was absolutely beautiful.

The minister started the ceremony off with prayer, May God the Father, the Son, and the Holy Spirit, bless, preserve and keep you; the Lord mercifully grant you the riches of his grace, that you may please him both in body and soul, and, living together in faith and love, may receive the blessings of eternal life. Greetings everyone, today we are here to witness the union of Kyra and Daron and the union of Trice and JayVon, if anyone under the sound of my breath has good reason as to why either of these couples should not be wed in holy matrimony, speak now or forever hold your peace."

"I believe both of the brides have written their own vows, so Kyra, please begin as you place the ring on Daron's finger."

Tears began slowly falling down Kyra's face, then she said, "Daron, when we met two and a half years ago, I could and did not image our lives being totally intertwined with one another, but this past two and a half years have been nothing short of amazing, I'm honored you chose me to be your wife, your homie, your forever lover, friend and the mother of your child, I love you and I promise to love, cherish, and honor you as long as there is breath in my body. I love you."

The minister then looked at Trice and said, 'Trice, your turn."

"Trice then turned to JayVon, and said, "My love, who would have thought that we'd be here, especially after how we met?" Everyone who knew how they met. began laughing, then she continued, "You came into my life at a time where I was almost at my lowest and you helped me to realize the queen that resided in me, you came into my world and showed me what true, unwavering, unconditional and non-judgmental love is. I will forever love you, support you, and stand beside you not only as your wife, but as your friend and biggest supporter."

The minister then looked at JayVon and said, "JayVon, it's your turn."

Jay turned to Trice then said, "Trice, we met under the most unusual circumstances, then hid our relationship from my brother and your best friend for the longest, you filled a void in my life that I didn't realize was missing until I met you. You understood me in ways no one else has ever understood me. You are a rare gem and I'm glad I was blessed to find you. I promise that as your husband I'm going to continue to support you, love you, build with you and be the sunshine you need in the midst of any storm you may face. I love you, I cherish you and I promise to never disrespect you or our union."

"Daron, you're up," the minister said. "Kyra, you are the blessing I never knew I needed in my life, since meeting you, every aspect of my life has amplified for the better since you came into my life. As your husband I promised to cherish, love, respect and support you. You are my rib, you were made just for me, and I promise from this day forward, you come first, and I will spend the rest of my life making sure you want for nothing. I love you."

"Kyra, do you take Daron to be your lawfully wedded husband?"

"I sure as hell do!!"

"Daron, do you take Kyra to be your lawfully wedded wife?"

"I sure do."

"Trice, do you take JayVon to be your lawfully wedded husband?"

"Hell yes!"

"JayVon, do you take Trice to be your lawfully wedded wife?"

"I do with all my heart."

"With the powers vested in me I now pronounce the two couples husband and wife, gentlemen, you may now salute your bride."

"Kyra, I noticed you said something about a child, you got something to tell me?" I whispered in her ear.

"I think I'm pregnant, but nothing concrete yet as I haven't taken a test."

I picked her up in one quick move, she was about to make me a father!! For the rest of the evening we celebrated one another, we celebrated love, life, and friendship. We hope you have enjoyed this short holiday story, but please know this is nowhere near the end of the Anal Assassin nor the Anal Princess, in fact, this is only the beginning.

G.B.D.s Kryptonite

Kryptonite is defined as a strong love and desire for something or someone. Something or someone you are unable to stay away from. Something or someone who make you weak

I'm convinced we have all been in a situation where someone was our kryptonite or we were someone's kryptonite. For me, my first love was my kryptonite and I was his. As a matter of fact, the first time we slept together he told me my pussy was his kryptonite.

Close to 20 years later, we are each other's addiction, we are great together but bad for each other...Julius is a culmination of men I've dealt with over the years, as are the rest of the men of the Initiation series. Marie is all me, as well as all of the women of the Initiation/ The Freak in Me series.

No relationship is perfect or even close to perfect as everyone is flawed, but real love and being truthful can conquer anything and everything. We at Rose Antrum Empire are big on Black Love which is why these characters of Initiation and The Freak in Me were created. We create characters who live the lives we envision, young, black, successful business owners who are about creating generational wealth and leaving legacies.

We hope you enjoy this short which introduces you to Brotha Great Black DIck and Soror Kryptonite. Be sure to look out for their full novels coming in 2026 as the lineup for 2024 is a bit hectic.

Love is love and we love us some love, especially Black Love...hope you enjoy it! And please, don't forget to check out the rest of the books in the Initiation/Freak in Me series that's already out, Initiation, The Freak in Me & An Anal Christmas.

The Rose Antum Empire team signing out,

Rocky Rose, Autumn Antrum, Saige the Gemini,

Brelynn Byrd, Salt, Keisha King & Ashlei Banxxx.

His dick has always had me balled up in the fetal position after we finished making love. His dick had to be modeled after Black Jesus' cause it was pure perfection, it was the perfect length & the perfect width. Fully erect, Julius' penis was an outstanding fourteen inches long and I'm not going to lie to y'all, the very first time we were intimate with one another, I was scared shitless! Who in their right mind would willingly suck and fuck a dick that could rearrange your insides?! I'm pretty sure he's done knocked my uterus, spleen, colon, and other organs all out of whack, but I promise you one thing, it'll be a cold day in hell before I willingly stop fucking with him and fucking him, he'd be a hard act to follow.

Ever since Julius and I met we've been damn near inseparable, we travel together, our favorite place being Hedonism in Jamaica. We make every holiday extra freaky and extra special in our own little way. Black Love Day and

Valentine's Day are two of the holidays we make sure we go all out for, I mean they are the two holidays dedicated to love right?!

Now y'all know what sorority and fraternity we're both in so you know anything we do, we have to add some spice to it, all naughty and not an ounce of nice. Seeing as though Julius and I were just in Ochos Rios for the double wedding of our friends, Trice and JayVon and Kyra and Daron, we opted to spend a week in Mexico at the Desire Riviera Maya Resort, sun, drinks, sex and more sex. We arrived in Mexico on a hot ass Saturday night, we purposely took a night flight so we could start this vacation off on a high, literally and figuratively, you know we had to get our mile high points in, so of course we had a few sessions in the bathroom on the plane. We were instantly greeted by our private driver at the airport and once we got into our car, we had him put the partition up and got our freak on inside of the car. I started out by slowly giving Julius head while he fingered my already dripping wet pussy, he then laid me on my back and began eating my love box while fingering my ass, I was in sexual bliss. While he kept two fingers in my ass, he gently slapped his hard dick onto my clitoris, which sent a violent orgasm ripping through my body. He finally entered me and began slowly stroking me, he knew just the right tempo to get me completely open, and open I was 'cause within the first five minutes, I was squirting all over him and the windows of the car. I gripped both of my breasts as orgasm after orgasm ripped through my body.

"That's my very good, bad girl, did you enjoy yourself?"
"You know I did, and you know I'm only this bad when it comes to you."

"You better be. Listen baby girl, I know we've been on the outs a bit lately, almost to the point of hating one another, but I'm really hoping that this week will bring us back to a place where we love one another and hopefully within the next year or so we could be the next couple that walks down the aisle and join our other fraternity and sorority brothers and sisters in the marriage club."

"Julius, I love you and I want us to work but I can't do this shit on my own. It takes two people to be in a relationship, I don't know when we got off track with one another but if you feel as if being with me brings you more pain than happiness, then I'd rather you be happy with someone else than miserable with me."

"You don't make me miserable Marie, I just feel as if I don't do it for you anymore, and if I'm being completely honest with myself and with you, imagining you with someone else doesn't sit right with me. I want you and only you, we have too much skin in the game to just give up on one another, and I'm willing to do whatever it takes to show you how serious I am about you and us."

Just as I was about to respond, we pulled up to our resort. We were greeted by the bellhops who were dressed in black suits and were standing with glasses of champagne for Julius and I, then the head of concierge greeted us and said, "Buenas tardes, my name is Diego, and I'll be your personal concierge for the duration of your stay here at Desire Riviera Maya Resort, whatever you need, I will be glad to assist."

I responded, "Thank you Diego, I'm Marie and this is Julius, I promise you we won't be much of a bother to you while we're here, we'll most likely be spending a lot of time in our room."

"No worries señora, I will be at your beck and call for the week."

Diego grabbed our bags from the car, and led us to our penthouse suite. When we got to your suite, there were magenta, yellow and silver rose petals all over the room and bathroom floors, there were also the same colored flowers in multiple vases around the room.

I looked at Julius and said, "You had something to do with this, didn't you?"

"I told you I want us to reconnect on this trip and what better way to do that than to show you love with your sorority colors? I mean, that's how we connected in the first place, isn't it?"

"I swear I love you, you always put so much thought into the smallest gestures," I told him before kissing him.

"Do either of you need anything before I leave?"

"Nah, I think we're good for right now, thank you for everything so far Diego," Julius responded.

As soon as Diego was gone, Julius made sure the door was locked, then he came towards me and picked me up, I wrapped my legs around him, and kissed him deeply and passionately. He gently placed me on top of the bar, kneeled down and began eating my pussy.

"Fuck Julius!" I wrapped my legs around his neck as he feasted on me, gently grabbing a handful of his locs as he was bringing me to orgasm heaven and I was enjoying every moment of it. Orgasm after orgasm ripped through my body and Julius seemed to have no plans on letting up anytime soon, that was until I squirted all over him.

"Damn baby, a heads up would have been nice."

"I'm sorry love, I couldn't give you a heads up, I could barely catch my breath, you know when your tongue is on any part of my body, it's an orgasm party over here."

He laughed then said, "Let's shower and go grab something to eat, I know you're hungry."

"You know me so well."

We showered, got dressed, and walked around the resort to find a restaurant we thought we'd like. We settled at the Jacuzzi Bar, the vibe was right, it was giving very much sensual and sexual seduction as it was clothing optional. We ordered drinks and small appetizers and immediately got into the 30-person hot tub. There were about five other couples already in the hot tub and we introduced ourselves and come to find out three of the five couples were around the same age as we were and they were all members of the same fraternity and sorority.

"So, Marie and Julius, where are y'all from?"

"I'm originally from Delaware, and Marie is originally from Massachusetts; how about all of y'all?"

Liam responded, "Dina and I are both from California, Evelyn and Carter are from D.C. Cole and Avery are from Rhode Island, Faith and Jackson are from Connecticut, and Mia and Mason are both from New Jersey."

"One of my frat brothers is from Jersey if I'm not mistaken, y'all crossed at the same time?"

"Yea, we all met within the first week of school, and we been bonded ever since, the ladies all went to school together on the east coast, met and all pledged Delta Pi Psi together, it was like we were all meant to meet one another when we did."

"That's what's up, how ironic we come all the way to Mexico and meet new fraternity brothers and sorority sisters?! Small world, isn't it?"

Marie responded, "We're going to have to make sure we stay in contact and link y'all with the rest of our crew, we're going to have to invite y'all to the DyNasty Pleasure Palace, we have a little bit of everything there, swingers club, adult toy store, we have an adult playground, it's definitely a vibe."

"Oh, that sounds like it's right up our alley," Cole said, winking at Avery.

"Listen, whenever y'all are ready to visit, hit me so I can make sure you're taken care of from beginning to end, you'll get the VIP treatment."

As the drinks started flowing, we all started getting a little more comfortable around one another, and the more comfortable we got, the friskier we got with our significant others. Julius lifted me onto the side of the hot tub, pulled my bikini bottoms to the side and began slowly licking my pussy. I grabbed a handful of his locs as orgasms ripped through my body. I made eye contact with Evelyn and motioned for her and Carter to join us. I was attracted to them when I first laid eyes on them.

Evelyn was already fully nude and her DD breasts and round ass had me dripping before we got into the hot tub. They came over to where Julius and I were and Carter immediately placed my head to his center and I was looking straight at his ten inch dick, mouth salivating like a dog with a steak in front of it. Evelyn began sucking Julius' dick but made sure to keep eye contact with me as I began sucking Carter's dick.

Crazy to say this to y'all but I could tell Julius wasn't enjoying himself with Evelyn on his dick, his facial expressions said all I needed to know. Carter on the other hand was thoroughly enjoying the feel of my lips and tongue on his dick because not even ten minutes in, his eyes were rolling in the back of his head, his dick began to pulsate, so I knew he was about to cum hard, but I was definitely not going to be swallowing his kids tonight. I motioned for Evelyn to come over so she could suck, swallow or be drizzled by her man's man potion, and I went over to finish Julius off like he so desperately needed.

"Hey y'all, I just airdropped you my number just in case we don't see you before we leave, we want to keep in touch with everyone," Julius told the crew before he picked me up.

"We're having a small get together tomorrow evening, I'll send y'all the information, clothes optional, it's going to get buck wild, so think about coming through," Liam told us.

"We'll think about it and let y'all know," I told them before being carried back to our room.

As Julius had me on his back I began kissing his neck and playing with his ears because our episode in the hot tub didn't end how either of us had hoped so I took it as a personal challenge to make sure my man went to bed with a smile on his face.

By the time we got back to our resort Julius' dick was rock hard, standing at attention so we got into the private elevator that led right up to our room and we started the party right in the elevator. I squatted in front of him, took his dick out and started out by just sucking the tip of it. He put his head back and his eyes rolled into the back of his head in pure ecstasy, I popped a mint into my mouth to bring him added pleasure to my already wet and warm mouth. My goal was to get him to cum before we made it to our room, and dare I say, the mission was most certainly accomplished.

He helped me stand back up then picked me up and carried me over to the couch, I laid on the couch and he began taking the little bit of clothes I had on right off me. Julius then said to me, "Come sit on daddy's face, my locs and beard need to be moisturized."

The raspiness of his voice turned me the fuck on, my pussy instantly started dripping. I straddled his face, and began grinding my hips on his face. His tongue glided in and out of my pussy like I was his favorite dessert, and his middle finger glided in and out of my ass hole, he was bringing me to a whole different level of ecstasy. Just as an orgasm was about to overtake me, we heard our doorbell ring.

"Whoever the fuck it is, please leave,

we're busy and need not be interrupted. Whomever it was at the door clearly got the hint because the knocking stopped and Julius and I got back to pleasing one another. Julius sucked on my clit slowly then reached one of his hands up to one of my breasts and began caressing it. Between him sucking my clit, his tongue massaging the inside of my pussy, one of his fingers in my ass, I could no longer hold back and the most intense orgasm I'd ever experienced in my life ripped through my body something vicious.

"Babyyyyy!!" I screamed out.

"Oh, I'm not even close to being done with you, that was just the beginning. Meet me on the balcony in two minutes," he told me before smacking my ass.

I had to sit on the couch for a quick minute to allow my heart rate to get back to almost normal and for my legs to not feel like rubber before I could meet him anywhere. As I was making my way to the balcony I noticed there was a delivery at our door, which is what whomever was knockin' at our door was trying to bring in for us.

"Baby, I think Trice and JayVon sent this ridiculously large bouquet of flowers to us, it's my fraternity colors mixed with your sorority colors."

"Is there a card attached?"
"Not that I can see."

"I'll talk to Trice tomorrow to see if she sent it, those flowers are the last thing on my

mind tonight," I told him, looking him up and down in all of his nakedness.

"Well Ms. Baxter, what exactly is on your mind tonight?"

"You and I in a few different positions all around this villa of ours, and you filling up my other two holes, Mr. Duncan."

"Is that right?"

"Indeed it is, now are you going to put those flowers down or are we going to talk about them for the rest of the evening?"

He placed the vase in the middle of the table, reached out his hand for mine, which I gladly took and he led me to the balcony. About five feet from where we were standing there was a tripod set up with a camera, this was about to be a trip to remember. Julius had the wireless remote and pressed record on it, and almost instantly I turned into the porn star that had been secretly hiding on the inside for the longest.

I started seductively dancing my way to where Julius was standing, making sure we were still in the view of the camera. I dropped to my knees and began fingering myself while maintaining eye contact with Julius, twenty seconds later I began squirting all over the place.

"Damn baby, bring your fine ass over here so daddy can fill your asshole with this dick."

"Okay daddy, now you're speaking my language," I told him as I crawled over to where he was. I stopped directly in front of him and took as much of his dick in my mouth as I could fit, cause like I told y'all earlier, my man was hung, like fourteen inches rock hard type hung.

I sat on one of the chairs on the balcony and scooted all the way to the edge. I needed and wanted to feel Julius fill my hole with all of him. Julius kneeled down, ate my pussy and my ass because he enjoyed eating me out for his own pleasure just as much as I enjoyed sucking his dick for more of my own pleasure. I was able to comfortably take about eight inches of Julius in my ass, anything more, I was going to need my ass reconstructed. As Julius was digging my ass out, he was simultaneously fingering my pussy and rubbing my clit, he was bringing to a different sexual atmosphere.

An hour and a half later, we both came multiple times and were drained, so we hopped in the shower together and we went straight to bed.

The Next Morning

As soon as Julius and I woke up there was breakfast waiting for us in our kitchen, Diego wasn't playing around, he was on point with everything.

"Babe, how long have you been planning this trip? You've been on point with all of the details and everything."

"Probably for about a month or so, but you know I had to enlist your girls to help with some of the details."

"I figured as much," I said laughing, then said, "do you think you want to go to the get together the crew we met last night are having tonight?"

"Nah, I'm good, I have something sexy planned for us this evening and I'm not changing the plans, so we'll catch them at a different time."

"Was it just me or was something a little off with them?"
"Something was definitely off with them, I just can't put my finger on what it is, and the fact that ol girl couldn't suck dick to save her life makes me wonder how the fuck she even made it through initiation for Delta Pi Psi."

"Why was I thinking the exact same thing last night?! I don't know about any other chapters of DPP but I know for damn sure my chapter was the best."

We showered, put our robes on and went to partake in the heavenly smelling breakfast that was prepared for us. Grits, oatmeal, sausage, bacon, eggs, breakfast potatoes, cranberry juice, orange juice and herbal tea was the spread they had for us and I'd be lying if I said we didn't pig out on all of it.

"Babe, I'm thinking we can keep it light today, chill in the room, maybe I can book a couple's massage for us, so we can be relaxed and ready for what I have planned tonight."

"Sounds good to me my love, you wore my ass out last night, literally and figuratively. I need to soak in the tub after I eat, so I can be loose before the massage."

"That sounds like a plan. I'm going to see what games are on, I'll be in the living room."

"*Do you need anything before I go soak?*"

"*No love, I'm good, I should be asking you if there is anything you need?*"

"*No, I'm good but I do want to talk to you about something when I get out of the tub.*"

"*Am I in trouble or something?*"

"*No, nothing like that, I know this week is supposed to be a week of us reconnecting, so I just want to talk about how we can reconnect and what we need from one another in order to make this relationship work.*"

"*Got it, well go ahead and soak so we can have this conversation.*"

Having this conversation with Julius was making my stomach turn. I'm not too sure if spending a week in Mexico having crazy sex with one another was going to be the solution to our underlying issues. I took my bath and allowed my body to soak for about forty-five minutes.

When I got out Julius was sitting at the bar with three drinks sitting in front of him.

"You have to drink in order to have this conversation with me?"

"No, but I need a drink to calm my nerves. I know we haven't been on the same page lately, and I take blame for that, I've been distant, trying to figure life out."

"Can you see a future with me?"

"I can, I feel as if you are my rib."

"Do you want a future with me?"

"Absolutely, I want to marry you, I want to have children with you."

"So what the fuck is the deal with you being ridiculously distant and making me feel as if the issues between us was something I did?"

"Marie, we've been rocking together for years, you are the first and only woman I've come across who I yearn for, the only one who can satisfy my every need and desire. You are the one and only woman for me, shit, you're the only woman I've dealt with who can keep up with me sexually. I can't and won't lie to you, part of me being distant is the fact that I kinda met someone else one night at the club, it wasn't intentional but our vibe was kinda dope, and we've been talking ever since the night we met."

"What in the entire fuck are you trying to tell me right now Julius?"

"I'm telling you that for a brief moment I thought I wanted to end things with you, but in talking and getting to know this new chick, I realized that you are the only woman for me."

"I think we need a break, I think we need to take some time apart and figure out if being together is the best thing for the both of us. Apparently I'm not enough for you because you're meeting new bitches at the club that I'm part owner of."

"Marie, I don't think taking a break is what we need, I booked this trip for us so we can reconnect, I don't want anyone else but you."

"Bullshit!! If I was the only one you wanted, you wouldn't have been entertaining other bitches; a break is definitely what we need and it's starting today, I'm booking a flight to go back home today," I told him heading to our room to start packing my suitcase.

"Marie! Please don't go back home. I really think we can use the remainder of our time here to figure this out and make things right between us. This is my fuck up where we are concerned and I'm hell bent on making it right, but I can't make it right if you leave."

"Did you sleep with her?"
He hung his head low, avoided eye contact with me then said, "Yes, we've slept together a few times, but I was always thinking of you when I was with her."

"Say less, let's take a month or two off, you can do whatever it is you were feeling like *you were missing with me, and once the two months are up, we can meet to see if being with one another is what we both want."*

     "Are you going to sleep with someone during our time apart?"
"I don't know, it's not on the forefront of my mind. I'm taking this time to focus on me and try to figure out why the man I've been head over heels in love with for over five years suddenly feels the need to fuck other bitches instead of being a man and telling me what's goin on with him and our relationship."

     "If it's any consolation every time she and I slept together, I was only thinking about you."

     "Negro please!!!! What kind of bullshit is that to tell me? That's like if I fucked someone else and tell you that when I was fucking him I was thinking of you the whole time. How the fuck would that sound to you?"

"I understand Marie, I do, I don't know why I do the shit I do, but I want you to know she can't hold a candle to you, she can't fuck me like you do, she can't suck me like you do, she's not even on your level when it comes to sex."

"You clearly have some underlying issues that you need to get a hold of, and I suggest you do it within the next two months cause on the thirty second day, your ass is either going to be grass or our relationship will be stronger than ever. I highly suggest you dig deep and seek whomever or whatever you need to seek to get your shit together," I told him before lifting my suitcase off the bed and heading to the door.

"I can't believe this mothafucka had the entire audacity to cheat on me! Like yo! I do everything for this man, cook, clean, entertain, suck his dick when he wants, shit, I even wake him up to breakfast and head, and everything *still ain't enough cause men like him are greedy and always want more,"* I said aloud to myself.

Diego saw me descending in the elevator and he met me as soon as the elevator hit the bottom floor and the doors opened.

"Señorita Marie, is everything alright?"

"No Diego, everything isn't alright, I need a car to take me to the airport like twenty minutes ago."

"Si señorita, there is a black truck outside, Señor Julius has a car on standby, the driver will take you wherever you need to go."

"Thank you Diego, you're a lifesaver. I thank you for everything you've done on this short lived trip of mine. Maybe in a month or so when I come back I'll get to see you again."

"Safe travels señorita, hope to see you soon."

The driver of the truck saw me coming so he hopped out and opened the back door for me, put my suitcase in the truck and took me to the airport. On the way to the airport I found a flight back home, I wasn't caring about the price or anything, I needed to get out of Mexico and fast. I had about twenty minutes to get to the airport and make it through security and to my gate to board, before I'd be sitting at the airport for the next flight which was in another three hours. I didn't want to chance Julius coming here and trying to talk me out of leaving.

Back in Atlanta...

As soon as I touched down in Atlanta, before even leaving the airport, I sent an S.O.S. text message to my sister grouper and asked them to meet me at my house as soon as they were available. When I got home, Trice and Akira were already there.

"Sis, what's up? Why are you back from Mexico already? Are you feeling okay?" Trice asked, rushing to me before I got out of the car.

"Did y'all know that Julius has been fucking some random bitch he met at the club?"

"Our club? As in the DyNasty Pleasure Palace?"

"Yup, the one and only," Akira asked.

"Since the fuck when? And to answer your question, no we didn't know, you know damn well we would have told you the moment we found out," Trice responded.

"He told me this morning. He said he set the Mexico trip up so we could reconnect because he's been hella distant lately. I wanted us to talk to air everything out and move forward with one another and that's when he told me he'd been fucking someone else."

"Damn sis, I really thought we'd all found good ones when we got with our men, has he called you since you left?" Akira asked.

"A million times, left voicemails and close to a hundred text messages. I'm so pissed right now I can't even bring myself to respond to him right now, he really has me vexed."

"We're going out tonight, you gotta shake this shit off, it's Valentine's weekend and you're not about to be cooped up in this house playing old school break up songs thinking of Julius," Akira said.

Akira and I brought our clothes with us, we're going to let the rest of the girls know what the plans are and we're going to act up tonight."

Trice sent a message to the rest of the girls to let them know that we were going out tonight, and the place to be was none other than the DyNasty Playground.

Kyra, Kiera, and Jade all responded that they'd be at my house within the next half hour. I swear having friends in your circle that refuse to let you sit and mope around because of your cheating ass man is the best.

The drinks began to flow, the weed was being rolled, my girls and I were getting right so we could get right in the club tonight. Tonight was also the DyNasty Pleasure Palace's annual Valentine's Threesome

Party, and because I desperately needed to get Julius off of my mind, I decided to partake in this year's festivities, and I'm hoping those who know Julius were there to report back to him.

"Ladies, tonight we are getting freaky, and I'm not talking about the married and tied down type of freaky, I'm talking about the type of freaky we were when we were in college going through our initiation for Delta Pi Psi," Trice told all of us while hand us shot glasses full of Hennessy.

"Sistas, tonight I'm going to do something I've never done before, I'm actually going to engage in our annual Valentine's Day Threesome, I need to get Julius out of my mind tonight and I think being in between two fine ass men, with a dick in my pussy and one in my mouth is just what the doctor ordered."

"Umm, Sis, you know I love you and I'm normally with all the shits, but do you think it's wise to do that? Aren't you and Julius still together?" Jade asked.

"Actually, we're not. I told him this morning that I think we needed to take about two months apart so he can get his shit together, so from today until two months from now, I'm single and I'm 'bout to do a hell of a lot of mingling."

The girls and I got dressed in our sexiest lingerie, I of course had on lingerie that left absolutely nothing to the imagination, I was ready to act up tonight and have all of my holes filled.

"Say less, y'all ready? Our driver for the evening is outside and we have him until he drops the last one of us off," Trice told us.

We all got into the Denali XL and made our way to the DyNasty Pleasure Palace. Of course since we're the owners, we went in through the back, we dropped our coats off into the owner's suite and headed to the main level in our personal elevator.

As soon as we got off the elevator two of our bartenders greeted us at the elevator with glasses of our favorite drinks. I had an amaretto sour, Trice had a hennessy and coke, Akira had a straight hennessy, Jade, Kiera and Kyra all had vodka and cranberry.

"Ladies, it's time for me to act up, I'll see ya when I see ya!" I told them before going to find two fine ass men to fuck my brains out for the night.

I walked around the club, getting turned on by seeing all of the couples that brought a third party to the party with them and the couples that met a single companion there at the club that they wanted to invite into their bed for the night, but I, however, wasn't as lucky. Even though I said I wanted to get Julius back for fucking some random that he had the audacity to meet at my club, the little angel on my shoulder told me not to engage in anything with anyone tonight, so I went back to the owner's suite and drank until the rest of the girls showed up to leave.

"Damn bitch, you must've enjoyed yourself, we ain't see you all night," Jade said as she and the rest of the ladies came into the owner's suite.

"I wish I could say I did enjoy myself, Julius has been on my mind all evening, I hate to admit this, but I miss his ass."

"You're probably going to see him when you go home tonight, he sent me a text message saying he's back in the states," Trice told me showing me the message he sent her.

"If he knows what's good for him, he won't show up at my house tonight, I meant what I said when I told him that we needed this time apart."

"So what are you going to do if he's at your place tonight?"
"I'm going to kindly ask him to leave and go on about my business. If I left Mexico earlier today, he should know by now that I'm serious about us taking a two month break to see if being together is something we both want or if we need to find love elsewhere."

"Sis, come here," Kiera said.
I walked over to the computer to see what she wanted.

"So, since earlier today I've been trying to find out who this random broad is that Julius met here and has been fucking. I know he's not here often but we all know that security keeps tabs on when any of our men are at the club without us. I was able to pull the camera footage from the last night he was here by himself, and I think I may have found the mystery woman in question, and you won't believe this shit, this bitch has the audacity to have our colors on, which is the ultimate disrespect."

"This chick is a sister? He didn't mention that to me this morning, her being a Deep Diva makes this shit even worse. I don't know if I can forgive him for this."

"I wonder if she's a real Deep Diva or if she's just reppin' the colors," Akira said aloud.

"I know one thing, by tomorrow morning, we'll know who this heifer is and everything about her," Trice said.

"Let's go y'all, staying here and looking at this shit is making me pissed all over again. You know what's crazy? I've been head over heels in love with this man for over five years and I haven't thought for once to step out on him. I don't even have guys in my phone to call just to fuck, ain't that some shit?"

"Sis, I promise you, ain't shit out here, I know I can speak for all of us when I say it's best to take this next two month to focus on yourself and hopefully Julius does the same, if he's smart, and when two months pass, the both of you will be stronger as individuals so you'll be unfuckwithable as a unit. We all want to see you happy, whether it's with Julius or with someone else," Akira said to me.

"I hear you. Let's go, I'm tired, horny and irritated, I'm sorry I dragged y'all here with me tonight for nothing."

"Fuck that, you needed to get out of the house, and that's what we did, you being here was better than you being in the house playing some sad ass love songs. We're not going home, I'm hungry so we're going out to eat," Trice said.

"How we going out to eat and we all have on some very scantily clad lingerie?" I genuinely asked.

"We can keep our coats on, I'm hungry and I'm not taking no for an answer, so let's go! You know how I get if I don't eat."

"I know, let's go."

We found a late night soul food spot that was still open, we were seated, and ordered our drinks, and not even ten minutes later, all of our significant others walked through the door.

"I know this is not a damn coincidence. Which one of you bitches told the men where we were?"

"My bad Marie, Justice asked what we were doing after the club, I mentioned to him we were going to eat, and I shared my location with him. We've been working on getting our relationship back on track as well."

"It's all good sis, I just didn't expect to see Julius here, that's all."

"I can ask them to leave if it'll make you feel better," Akira responded.

"Nah, it's cool, I haven't seen my
brothers in a while, I can ignore Julius, it's not
a problem.

"Marie, can we go outside and talk
please? I know you've been ignoring my calls
and text messages."

"Nah, I'm good, I said all I needed to say
earlier today."
"Marie, this two month break bullshit isn't
sitting right with me."

"Why isn't it? Is it because you now
have a free pass to fuck your new friend without
having to think about me? I'm legit giving you a
free pass to fuck for two months."

"That's not what I want. I want you, like
I told you earlier, you're the only woman for
me."

"Julius, if I were really the only woman
for you, you wouldn't have met this random
broad at the club, a broad who was wearing my
sorority colors I might add, and you wouldn't

have been fucking her for the past month and a half! Please get the fuck outta my face with your bullshit today, I'm so done and over you."

"FUCK!!" He yelled in obvious frustration. "Hey y'all, I'm going to bounce, I just called a car to bring me home, I'll text you when I get in. I done lost my appetite," I told my girls.

"Dammit! This is all my fault," Akira said, now visibly upset.
"It's not your fault sis, I'm not blaming you, I promise I'm not."

I left the restaurant with Julius standing there looking like he just lost his best friend. I needed time to get my mind right and my thoughts together. At this very moment I was about ninety percent sure that Julius and I's relationship was done for good. I love this man with every fiber in my body but the fact that he allowed some random chick to be intimate with him in a way that was only supposed to be for me, I felt like he betrayed me in the worst way and I'm not sure I'll ever be able to trust him again.

When I got home I poured myself a tall glass of Hennesy on the rocks, no chaser, took that to the head, took a nice long hot shower, and masturbated myself to sleep.

A Month Later

I stopped all communication with Julius the night he came to the restaurant and wanted to have a conversation with me. I needed to take time for myself to figure out if I could forgive him and move on with him or if I just wanted to say fuck it all and throw away the past five years we've spent together as a couple. According to my brothers, he's been staying to himself and supposedly working on himself too. I would love to think that this break has made me forget the betrayal, but I feel like Lance in the *Best Man*, when he kept having visions of Mia and Harper fucking, I keep having visions of

Julius and that random chick in bed together and her sucking his dick, it pisses me off.

I decided to send a text to Julius for him to meet me at the coffee shop we go to at least three times a week. I wanted to talk to him to see where his head was at.

"Hey Julius, I know it's been a while since we've spoken, but I wanted to see if you're available to meet me at the coffee shop we normally go to, I just want to talk to you and see what your thoughts are and where your head is at. Hit me back when you see this."

Two minutes later, he responded, "Hey love, I can meet you there in ten minutes if that works for you. You're right, it has been a while and I've been wanting to talk to you as well. Love you."

"See you in ten," was all that I replied. When I got to the coffee shop Julius was already there sitting at the table we always sat at. I can't and won't lie, just seeing him from ten feet away made my heart pound a little faster, the butterflies in my stomach were going crazy, he was so fine and I missed him terribly. When he saw me approaching him, he stood up to greet me.

"Hey love, you look beautiful as always. I ordered your normal tea and I also got you two cinnamon rolls like you like."

"You know me so well and sometimes I can't stand it, but thank you."

"Baby girl, let's be honest with one another, we belong together, we know one another almost better than we know ourselves, and I'm talking in and out of the bedroom. You know you are my rib, and I know you're the only woman for me."

"Have you been in contact with or been sleeping with your sidepiece?"

"No, I deaded that the morning we had our falling out in Mexico, she's not worth me losing you over, and she's not a member of your sorority, I did my homework on her, but she did say something about wanting to cross soon, but just know, when I was dealing with her, she was not a part of Delta Pi Psi."

"Oh, I know, I did my homework on ol girl, you better thank Black Jesus that she isn't a member of my organization because if she was, you'd be pushing up daisies."

"SO, the million dollar question, where do we go from here? Have you figured out if you want to be with me or is this where our story ends?"

"What do you want to do?"
"I want you and only you baby girl. You are my future wife, so I'm all in with you."

"Julius I love you and I've been in love with you for over four years. I envision a future with you, having your children, growing old with you, but the fact still remains that you betrayed me, how can I ever forgive you for that?

"I wish I had the answer to that baby

girl, all I can tell you is that I'm here for you and only you. I won't ever step out on you again, you have my word on that. I am willing to do whatever it takes to show and prove to you that I'm yours and only yours."

I stood up, walked over to Julius and whispered in his ear, "You miss this lips around your dick, don't you?"

He gently grabbed me by my neck, then whispered to me, "You miss this dick rearranging your insides, don't you?"

"You know I do. You miss this pussy too, don't you?"
"You know I do, so what are we going to do about us missing one another?"

"You're going to come home with me so we can show one another how much we missed each other."

"Is my good girl going to be bad for me today?"

"You know she is, and you know she's only a bad girl for you."

"I just have one question before we leave."

"What's that?"

"Did you sleep with someone else while we took this break?"

"Nope, the night the girls and I went to the Palace, I thought about engaging in a threesome with two guys, but I couldn't get you out of my head. Instead, I sat in the owner's suite until the rest of the girls were done partying."

"Okay, let's go home and make up now, I've missed being inside of you."

When we got back to my place, Julius took me right in the front foyer, he laid me on the bench, took my clothes off, took his jeans off and entered me. I gasped loudly because even though he's been the only man I've slept with in the past five years, I still haven't gotten used to his width or length, I mean seriously, who can honestly say they can get used to their man and his fourteen inch penis?

He kept steady with slow strokes, sucking my breasts and gently choking me, just like I like it. He knew my body inside and out, there was no one who could do my body like him, and there was no one who could do his body like me. Our relationship went beyond the sex though, we motivated each other to grind harder, we have businesses that we're about to start together.

"Baby, you're about to make me cum again!"

"Cum all over daddy's dick baby. Oh yes, keep on cummin, your legs are shaking and everything."

"Babyyyy, you're about to break my pussy!!"

Just as Julius was about to respond, my doorbell rang.

"Who the fuck is interrupting us right now?" Julius yelled loud enough for whomever was at the doorbell to hear."

"Julius, I know you're in there, I can hear you! You need to come to this door right now!"

"Who the fuck is that Julius?"

"How the fuck am I supposed to know, I'm balls deep in your pussy right now."

I got up, put my clothes back on and went to see who the fuck was at my door. I swung my door open and said, "Is there something I can help you with?"

She responded, "You must be the infamous Marie, my name is Qortni."

"Yo, what the fuck are you doing here? How did you even find me here?"

"I've been following you since you broke things off with me, you must've blocked me too, I've been trying to contact you, I'm pregnant and the baby is yours!"

"Bullshit, I strapped up twice every time we fucked, and I always pulled out before nutting in the condoms, so there's no way possible you're carrying my seed."

"Yea, aight, we'll see when I hit your ass with the paternity test. Oh and Marie, just to let you know, he told me I was better than you."

I looked that bitch up and down and could do nothing but laugh, then I responded, "Ain't no damn way your little frail ass fucks or sucks my man better an me. You're out of your rabid ass mind."

"Julius, I love you and I thought you loved me too," Qortni said tearfully.

"Go ahead with that love bullshit, you already know everytime we slept together I always told you that Marie was the only one for me, now I'm telling you this right now, get the fuck on and don't come back here."

I closed the door with her standing there looking like a complete idiot.

"A fucking baby Julius?"

"Marie, it's not mine, and that's on my life. That chick is bugged out, believe me when I tell you, there's no way in hell that she's carrying my child."

You know what, I'm not going to let that chick ruin my mood. Let's go upstairs and finish what we started before we were so rudely interrupted.

Just as we were on our way up the stairs, we heard glass shattering. "I know this bitch didn't do what I think she did," I said aloud.

"Are your cameras on?"

"They're always on," I responded while going to my security room. Just as I suspected, this chick busted out the windows on both of our vehicles.

"I'll call the cops and file a complaint, babe, please don't think about getting revenge on this chick."

"Too late, she's definitely going to feel it, but I'm not focused on her right now, you go ahead and call the cops because as soon as they come and go, I'm devouring your dick, I don't take kindly to being interrupted when it's our nasty time."

"We hitting the shower once this mess is straightened out, you how we love our shower sessions."

"I'm going to set the camera up now, we're going to finish making the movie we started in Mexico."

"Speaking of Mexico, Liam and the rest of his crew hit me the other day, they said they'd be in Atlanta in like two weeks and wanted to know if we wanted to link with them while they're here."

"I'm not sure yet, can I get back to you on that? The vibe I got from them was a little off, I'll see what the girls think, did you mention it to the guys?"

"Yea, they said they'd be down to chill with them, to feel them out and get to know them."

"Cool, well listen, tonight it's all play time for us, we have a lot of make up sex to have, but come tomorrow, I want to run a business idea by you, something I think we should start together."

"Whatever it is, you know I'm game, we in this together and creating generational wealth, right?"

"You know it baby."

A Year Later

"Julius, where do you see us in the next five years?"

"I see you being my wife, we'll have a house full of children, thriving businesses and you and your sorority sisters having a chain of DyNasty Pleasure Palace in different states. My brothers and I have a chain of our adult toy stores in different states as well."

"You want to marry me one day?"

"Stop acting like you don't know that already, I keep telling you that you're my rib, you were made especially for me and I believe I was made especially for you, now do me a favor and go get dressed, we're going for a ride and we have to leave within the next half hour."

"Where are you taking me?"

"If I told you it wouldn't be a surprise, now would it?"

"Okay, at least tell me what I should put on, casual, dressy, sexy?"

"Put on something sexy for daddy, I'm sure you're going to want to be sexy for what I have planned."

I showered quickly and popped the tags on this sexy all black jumpsuit. I didn't know what Julius had planned, but I knew whatever it was, I was going to be dressed for it. Once we got in the car, Julius had smooth jazz music playing, he was setting the mood and I was here for it. As we were approaching our final destination, he pulled out a satin blindfold and asked me to put it on. I hesitated for a moment but ended up obliging.

He helped me out of the car and as soon as I stepped out, I heard Musiq Soulchild's song 143 playing.

"Julius, what's going on here?"

"You'll find out soon enough, just a few more steps and you can take the blindfold off." Once I took the blindfold off, there were my sorority sisters and their significant others standing around a sea of rose petals the colors of my sorority.

"Julius, what's going on?"

"I told you from the moment we met six years ago that I was going to make you my wife, I told you that you were the only one for me, and I meant that." He then grabbed my hand and we walked to the center of the rose petals so we were surrounded by our loved ones.

"Marie LaPrea Baxter, would you do me the honor of being my wife?"

"You damn real I will!" I told him as he placed the black diamond and gold princess cut ring on my finger.

The waterworks were never ending, a year ago I couldn't imagine being engaged to Julius, shit, a year ago I wasn't even sure we'd still be together. A year ago he had this chick claiming to be pregnant by him and I was two seconds from cutting him off again, but who am I kidding? This man makes my heart skip beats, he still gives me butterflies, six years later, and he gets me like no one has ever before.

"Marie my love, you know you're my kryptonite, don't you?"

"I know that now, but do you know that you're my addiction?: An addiction that I never want to be cured from. I love you with my entire soul."

"*I'm going to make sure that you know everyday we're together how much you mean to me.*"

Being as though we were surrounded by our closest friends and family members, I thought this would be the perfect time to make the announcement that I'd been hiding for over two months now.

"Hey everyone, can I grab your attention for just a few minutes?"

Everyone got quiet and all attention was on me.

"Julius, my love, you have gone above and beyond proving your love to me. A year ago things were looking rather shaky between us, and there were times where I really wanted to be done with you but I knew in my heart of hearts that losing you would hurt me even more than whatever it was we were dealing with. With that being said, to my sorority sisters, my brothers and to the love of my life, I want you all to be the first to know that this soon to be Duncan party of two is going to be a Duncan party of four in seven months!!"

"Wait, party of four? Are you pregnant with twins?"

"Indeed I am my love, whatever water Trice was drinking, I think she gave it to me."

"Indeed I did sis, indeed I did!" Trice responded laughing.

"I can't wait to meet the two newest members of our family!" Akira shrieked with excitement.

Being the right person's kryptonite is such a dope feeling. Finding that one person who is serious about you and wants to spend their life with you, build with you and create timeless memories with you is an amazing experience. This isn't even close to being the end of our chapter, this is somewhere in the middle of it, but rest assured, you're going to hear from us again!

Make sure you stay tuned because GBD and Soror Kryptonite along with the rest of our crew will be having their books dropping soon! We hope you've enjoyed this glimpse into our lives. Bye bye for now! Oh and Happy Black Love Day, kisses! Xoxoxo

Soror Kryptonite

The Alluring Tigress: Qortni's Initiation

Qortni's Initiation

Having pussy this good should be a sin...I wonder if Jesus ever got tempted when he was out healing the sick, laying hands on people and out being perfect. Did he ever get an erection?

Never thought y'all would see or hear from me again after my book Bruised Never Broken came out with my letters to my exes and others last year, but here I am, in a whole different world, and if I'm being honest with y'all, I'm loving this new sorority life. I just crossed into Delta Pi Psi Sorority, Incorporated and babyy, it's the second best decision I've ever made in my life! Y'all know I've always wanted to be in a particular Divine 9 sorority but seeing as though I never finished college, that was a no go, so here I am, one of the newest members of the Beta Chapter of Delta Pi Psi erotic sorority!

If you've followed me throughout the years then you know I'm a sucker for men with *big dicks and hurricane tongues, so you know during my initiation process, I was spread eagle and all smiles. I came across DPP on one of the social media apps and I was intrigued to say the least, so I reached out to them, they told me they'd call me in a few days for a phone interview.*

"Hello, is this Ms. Monroe?"

"It is, may I ask who's calling?"

"This is Laniyah from Delta Pi Psi Sorority, I'm calling you in regards to your interest in the sorority."

"Ohh yes! That was quick, I just submitted my interest form two days ago."

"Yea, we don't play around, we had quite a few interest forms come in around the same time you put yours in. Is now a good time for you to talk?"

"It is."

"Ok, great, first question, what do you know about our organization?"

"Delta Pi Psi is an erotic sorority, and while they are an erotic sorority, they pride themselves on sisterhood, community service and education. One is not permitted to have a college degree to be a member but some type of vocational training is necessary."

"Excellent, I see you've done your research on us. Qortni, why do you want to join our organization?"

"I believe I embody the spirit and sexiness of Delta Pi Psi and if I may be completely honest, with the organization being erotic, that's right up my alley. I'm no stranger to community service as I serve the less fortunate in my community every holiday, and I'm a nationally certified phlebotomist."

"Very impressive, well on behalf of Delta Pi Psi, I invite you to complete the official application which will be emailed to you by the end of the business day, and once your application is reviewed you will either hear from me or one of the other ladies as to whether or not you will be invited to move on."

"Thank you so much Laniyah, I appreciate you and your time! Hope to hear from you soon!"

"You're most welcome, enjoy the rest of your day Queen!"

I ain't gon lie to y'all, I stalked my email for the rest of the day, and the moment that application hit my inbox, I filled it out, submitted everything they asked of me and sent it right back to them within an hour, I'd never been so sure of joining an organization.

Three days later as I was checking my emails I noticed an email from the organization and it read, *Greetings Ms. Qortni Monroe, on behalf of Delta Pi Psi Sorority, Incorporated, we'd like to extend you the invitation to join the Beta Chapter rush. Our first meeting will be held this Friday afternoon at four, the address is 3000 Dixwell Ave, Hamden, CT. If you have any* questions, please respond to this email and we'll get back to you at our earliest convenience.

"Ahhhh!!!!"

"What the hell are you screaming for?" My cousin Derrell asked.

"I just got invited to rush the beta chapter of Delta Pi Psi!!"

"That's that freaky ass sorority?"

"You know it!! D, please don't tell anyone about this, I'm supposed to keep this under wraps until I officially cross, I don't want to fuck this opportunity up."

"I got you lil cuz, you have nothing to worry about, my lips are sealed."

"I appreciate you big cuz, I really do."

"No doubt."

Friday morning...

I have no clue what the hell I'm wearing this afternoon and I still need to get my hair done! Okay Qort, you got this, you ain't new to this, you true to this. I went to my closet and grabbed three pantsuits that still had the tags on them. I hoped and prayed that I was still able to fit them, I'd been gaining a significant amount of weight over the past couple of months and most of my clothes that I had I'd given to my daughter. I knew I had a few hours to get my shit together, make sure my kids were fed, and were good, and I sent a text to my younger brother to see if he'd be available if I were gone for more than three hours to go check on the kids for me.

An hour before the meeting my stomach was in knots, nervous was an understatement, I was honestly kind of scared because I had no idea what I was getting myself into, but I was too far to turn back now.

I pulled up to the address given with twenty minutes to spare. I hated being late to anything, and if I got anything from my father, it was being on time was being late and being early was being on time, so I made it a point to be early to anything I was attending. Shortly after I parked, three other cars pulled up and in each car were at least 2 other women in it other than the driver.

"Qort, you seriously need some female friends, walking into this shit solo dolo ain't it," I said aloud to myself. After sitting in my car for another five minutes, I got out and headed inside the massive warehouse.

"Good afternoon and welcome Qortni, nice to finally meet you in person."
"Good afternoon queen, it's nice to meet you too, you must be Laniyah, your voice sounds familiar."

"Indeed I am, in a few minutes you will probably meet more of my sorority sisters and possibly my younger sister, Trice."

"I'm so excited, a little nervous but mostly excited about what's in store during this process."

"I hope you're ready! Take a seat anywhere you'd like, we're going to get started exactly at three."

I took a seat and some of the other ladies started coming in, we introduced ourselves to one another, exchanged phone numbers and waited for the meeting to start.

Exactly at three o'clock Laniyah began the meeting, "Greetings ladies, I'm glad you were all able to make it today, as you already know, I'm Laniyah, but you will be addressing me as Big Sister Squirt In Ya Face. Tonight we will cover a ton of information, please hold all questions until the end because chances are, they will be answered during this informational. First things first, if you are not a freak, if you don't love sucking dick, getting catcn out, or anal sex, then I'm going to kindly ask you to get up and leave, we will not judge you if you leave, but we'd rather have you leave now than have you starting the rush process and then you decide that this is not the sorority for you. We will give you thirty seconds to make up your mind and leave."

The room fell silent for exactly half a minute, none of the ladies left, then Laniyah continued.

"Well alright, with everyone still here, let's get down to business. We're going to keep this as short and to the point as possible cause I have a dick appointment in two hours and I refuse to be late. As you already know, Delta Pi Psi Sorority, Incorporated is an erotic sorority that isn't only centered around sexual pleasures, but also sisterhood, community service, and philanthropy. The Fearless Five that founded the sorority knew that none of the other sororities had what they were looking for so they set out to create a sorority that was one of a kind, and then DPP was birthed. When you become a sister, you become family, and we all know that some family members really ain't shit, but one thing we absolutely don't tolerate in this sorority is women sleeping with the significant others or spouses of our sisters."

"We don't condone our significant others sleeping with our sisters either," said another woman who was in a dope ass Delta Pi Psi sweatsuit. "I'm sorry y'all, I busted up in the meeting and didn't even introduce myself, my name is Trice, but you'll be calling me Big Sister Porn Star."

"By a show of hands, how many of you ladies in here have a significant other or husband?"

Two of the ladies raised their hands and simultaneously said, we're married."

"Okay so the two of you really need to think long and hard about whether or not this sorority is for you cause during your initiation process there will be a lot of fucking."

"We have and our husbands are cool with it, they are a part of Beta Delta Mu, Fraternity."

"So y'all just bout to be one freaky ass fraternity and sorority family, I ain't mad at it," Trice said laughing.

"Something like that, one of the ladies responded, rolling her eyes at Trice."

"Little lackey, I caught that eye roll, do we have an issue? Did I fuck your man or something?"

"As a matter of fact, you did," homegirl said with an attitude.

Trice started laughing, "What's his name?"
"Dwight Henderson."

"His dick clearly wasn't good cause I don't remember him."

"Or maybe your pussy was too wide open for you to actually enjoy him," homegirl shot back.

"On that note, you can exit stage left sweetheart, we don't need or want and won't tolerate the bullshit. You clearly came here with an agenda to start some shit and I promise you, it's not going to end well for you. From this day forward you are permanently banned from ever applying to Delta Pi Psi Sorority, Incorporated again, and I have half a mind to permanently ban you from ever attending any DPP events for the rest of your life, gather your shit and bounce!" Laniyah told ole girl.

"Well if she goes, I go, we came together and I ride for and with my sister," the girl sitting next to her stated.

"I'm not stopping you, now since you were a little nicer, as of right now, you can apply at a later time to join the sorority, but as for your sister, she's a reynolds," Laniyah responded.

Once the girls left, Trice said, "we're going to wrap this meeting up now, the energy is off because of that bitch. Keep your phones on and near you at all times, you will most likely get messages at the craziest times of the morning or night, your first initiation task will be sometime within the next few days. Any questions, feel free to email us cause yall ain't ready to have our numbers yet. Y'all are dismissed."

"One more thing before you leave, if you miss two or more initiation tasks, you will immediately be kicked off line, no exceptions or excuses," Laniyah added. "Qortni, stay behind for a moment if you can please; I want to talk to you."

My heart began to race, I wasn't sure what Laniyah could have wanted to speak with me about, I hope I didn't subconsciously do something to fuck my initiation up.

Once all the ladies left, Trice and Laniyah approached me.

"So, Qortni, we did a little digging into your background, you've been through hell and back in the past. What made you decide to pledge Delta Pi Psi?" Trice asked.

"I'm in a new place in my life, I've always wanted to be a part of a sorority but never finished college, and I truly believe I can thrive even further in my career being a part of a sisterhood such as this one."

"You have the spirit of a leader, and I realized that the day we had your phone interview. How would you feel about a private initiation? I feel like you are an Ace and you'd be the ace of the line, we have another meeting in a few days for some last minute applications that came in."

"Seriously? You want me as the Ace for our line? I'd be happy to be the Ace! As far as the private initiation, can I have some time to think about that? I wouldn't want the other women to feel a way if they don't see me at the initiation events."

"Just the answer we were looking for, you can't be a leader if you're only thinking about yourself, I'm looking forward to seeing how you perform and lead your line, Qortni." Trice said.

"I appreciate the both of you for this opportunity and I hope I do the sorority and our line justice."

"We have faith in you Qortni. Make sure to keep your phone by you and not on vibrate so you won't miss any messages or notifications. We will be sending you the date and time for our next meeting so you can meet the rest of the ladies that will possibly be joining the line," Laniyah responded.

"Will do, I thank you ladies again for this opportunity, looking forward to hearing from you soon."

"This is really happening, don't fuck this up Qortni, you better show up and show out during this initiation process," I said aloud to myself as I was leaving.

Three Days Later...

At exactly three o'clock in the morning my phone started singing to me, I knew it was none other than one of the big sisters from the sorority.

The message read, "*Good morning ladies, I hope you all are ready for your first initiation task. Please meet us at the warehouse at 4am where we had our initial meeting, please be prompt, if you're not on time, you will no longer be a part of this line. See you soon.*"

"Ok Qort, we have to be there in an hour, so you need to be here within the next half an hour," I said aloud to myself.

I got up, showered quickly and put on a t-shirt, a pair of sweatpants, and my sneakers. I checked in on my children to make sure they were good, and told the babysitter to text me if she needed anything while I was gone. I made it to the warehouse within fifteen minutes, so I still had a lot of time to kill. Instead of waiting in the car, I went to see if the warehouse was open, I can't imagine the big sisters not being there before us.

"Just as we expected, earlier than everyone else, hence why we have made you the Ace of the line," Laniyah told me.

"I'm taking all of this as seriously as I do my regular job, joining Delta Pi Psi is what I want so I'm going to do everything in my power to make sure I don't misstep."

"Spoken like a true leader, since you are here early, step into the first room in the back of the warehouse to your immediate left, the door should have your name on it, your first initiation task begins now," Trice said.

"Can't wait to see who or what awaits me in the back, see you ladies later!"
I walked to the back of the warehouse, spotted the room with my name on it, opened the door and lo and behold, there were three God body built men, as naked as Adam in the Garden of

Eden. Three men, different shades of chocolate and as hung as one of my arms.

"Are you ready for a night you'll never forget?" asked the brotha who was the complexion of a walnut.

"Baby, tonight I'm yours for you gentlemen to do whatever you like to and with me. I have three holes, I'm ready for y'all to fill them up."

The guy who was the shade of caramel then said, "take your clothes off, get on your knees and crawl over to us nice and slow."

I obliged, slowly and seductively taking off my sneakers, then my sweatpants, and lastly my shirt. I didn't like wearing underwear so I didn't put any on earlier. I got on all fours and began crawling to the men, stopped midpoint, laid on my back and spread my legs wide enough so they could see my pretty pussy. The shy brotha who hadn't yet said a word to me began stroking his already erect dick, and when he and I locked eyes, I began fingering my wet pussy. Just as I was about to climax I began rubbing my pussy so I could make myself squirt, and oh what an exhilarating feeling that was.

I got back on all fours and crawled the rest of the way to the men.

Mr. Caramel then said, "Come suck this dick baby, I want to see if you can fit all of it in that pretty ass mouth of yours."

"I'm always up for a challenge," I replied, getting on my knees on the bed to bless his dick with my lips. I began working my lips and tongue around his, what I assumed was at least thirteen inch, penis.

Shy dude stood behind me and put his thick ass dick inside my tight asshole. Now I know a lot of females don't like anal, but I love it, but shy brotha was definitely the largest penis I've ever had stuffed inside of my butt.

Mr. Nut slid underneath me and slowly inserted all ten inches of his dick inside of me, I gasped because I'd never had a threesome with three guys before and I promise you, each one of them had a dick larger than any guy I've ever slept with, y'all know what I'm talking about, and if you don't go back and read the *My Man My Abuser* series by my girl Rocky Rose.

Anyway, I was flipped from the North, SOuth, East and West in that bed by all three men. After a while I felt like I was a human compass. We moved the party from the bedroom to the main warehouse area where it seemed as if other women from my line were with their men of the evening.

"Well, well, it seems as if someone has had a rather exciting evening. Gentlemen, your services are no longer needed, you are free to leave the premises. You have five minutes to gather your belongings and exit the building. Qortni, we thank you for your participation in tonight's events, you are also free to go," said this mystery woman whom I'd never met before.

"I'm sorry, we haven't met, and I don't feel comfortable leaving the ladies here seeing as though I'm the Ace of the line."

"Sweetheart, I don't care if you're the Ace, the fifth or the damn Anchor, if one of your big sisters has told you that you're free to go, then that's what the hell it means."

Just as I was about to respond, Big Sister Squirt in Ya Face came from what seemed like out of nowhere and said, "Akira, cut your shit, you ain't been here but for a hot minute and you're causing unnecessary drama, what the hell is the issue?"

"I told the guys that were in the back room and this one right here that they were free to go for the evening and she was talking about she doesn't feel comfortable leaving since she's the Ace of the line, I don't even know who the hell told her that shit."

"Trice and I made the decision that she'd be the Ace and she was absolutely correct in telling you that because she's the Ace, she wouldn't be leaving the rest of her line behind. What the fuck is wrong with you?"

"I'm going to get dressed and join the other ladies while the two of you work through whatever it is you need to work through," I told them feeling hella uncomfortable.

"Ok, I'll come find you once we're done handling this issue, don't leave yet though."
"I'm not, first one in, last one out, you know I got this!"

Laniyah, Trice and Akira all walked to the back of the warehouse, opposite of where I was with the three guys who just stretched every hole in my body.

Twenty minutes later, the ladies came back, and Akira looked pissed as hell.
"Aye yoooo, gentlemen, we thank you for your services tonight. We kindly ask that you get dressed as quickly as possible and vacate the premises immediately, your rides back to your

starting point are outside waiting on you, and if you take too long to vacate, they will leave you and you'll have to use your two feet to get you home. Y'all ain't gotta go home but you gotta get the fuck outta here!" Laniyah told all the men in the building.

Ten minutes later and all the men were gone, no one else was in the building except for all of us ladies.

"Ladies, congratulations on completing your first initiation task, we hope you enjoyed yourselves. Y'all remind me of my line sisters and I when we were going through our initiation," Trice said to the group.

"I don't think they were as freaky as y'all though sis," Latrice said laughing.
Trice replied, "True indeed! I think we set the bar to a whole different level, but anyway, there was an incident earlier that we need to discuss. About half an hour ago one of the big sisters and one of the potential new members got into

a verbal spat. We are to respect each and everyone in this organizations, whether you are a member of Delta Pi Psi or if you're trying to be a member. My Soror and blood sister, Sista Squirt in Ya Face and I unanimously decided that Qortni will be the Ace of your line, as you all continue to go through this initiation process you will meet a plethora of Big Sisters. Earlier some of you met Big Sista Throat Doctor, now she and Qortni hadn't yet had the opportunity to meet but had words with one another, if there is an issue amongst ourselves, we handle it amongst ourselves, never in the presence of outsiders. The way Big Sis Throat Doctor handled herself tonight was totally inappropriate and since she decided to publicly embarrass Qortni, she will now publicly apologize to her."

Akira then stepped forward and said, "Good morning ladies, I want to first apologize to my line sister Trice, as well as my big sister Laniyah for acting out the way I did this morning. I now want to apologize to Qortni for blowing up on you the way I did, it was uncalled for, and I know how to conduct myself better. I accept full responsibility for any repercussions that may come as a result of my behavior. Qortni, I don't have an issue with you because I don't even know you. I honestly hope you can accept my apology." I ain't gon lie to y'all, I rolled my eyes a little and then responded, "I'm only accepting your apology because we're going to be sisters once my initiation is done, Black Jesus is still working on me, so we're good for now."

"Yo, I really like you Qortni, you shoot straight from the hip and don't be giving a fuck about people's thoughts or feelings, you're going to fit in perfectly with us!" Trice said laughing.

"Ladies, you are all dismissed, we thank you for showing up and showing out this morning, as always, get to your next destination safe and sound and remember to keep your *phones on so you will know when your next initiation task is," Laniyah told us.*

"Ladies, I just airdropped you all my phone number, if we're going to eventually cross the burning sands together, we need to hold each other accountable and make sure we all show up and show out during this initiation process."

Trice and Lanyiah both turned to Akira, looked at her and said simultaneously, "Now do you see why we made her the Ace, this line may end up being tighter than ours."

Before leaving the warehouse, I wanted to talk to Laniyah and Trice about their offer for my private initiation.

"Qortni, is everything alright? Everyone else has left already."

"Big SIsta Porn Star, I was wondering if I could talk to you and Big Sista Squirt In Ya Face for a moment?"

"Absolutely, what's up?" Laniyah said, joining us.

"I've had some time to think about your offer for my private initiation, if I agree to do it, would that mean that I can't participate in the initiation tasks with the rest of my line?"

"Not at all, you'd be able to do both if you choose. Now your private initiation would be more like a surprise type of thing, we'd know all the details, but you on the other hand would not, we want to see how you are when you're fully relaxed, not thinking about making a good impression on us so you can cross. It will entail sex, community service, stuff like that," Trice said.

"Now you have my attention, I'm game!"

"Great, you know to keep your phone on you at all times so you can get the notifications about the next group initiation task, I think the next one will be a community event seeing as though school will be starting in a few weeks, we're

going to partner up with our brother fraternity
and do a school supply drive."

"I'm all for it, Qort loves the kids!"
"Great, we'll be seeing you soon then Sis."

I was excited, I loved doing community
service, and being able to give back to the
children in my community was going to be a
dope event.

The Next Day...

"So Qort, how do you feel knowing that you're
about to be in an erotic sorority?"

"It's so dope D, but you know damn well
I can't talk about it with you."

"Trust me, I don't want to hear about your
sexapades, so please, spare me the details."

"I wasn't going to tell you anyway. I do
like the ladies I've met so far though, they're
cool as hell. I think we're going to get along just
fine."

"I still can't believe you out of all people
are joining a sorority, you and I both know you

don't really get along with women, so I'm curious to see how this shit is going to work out for you."

"I know, but I'm trying to change that. Do you think it's healthy for me to literally only hang with a bunch of men? You know I want to settle down and get married one day soon, and me hanging out with my male friends all the time is not going to put me in front of men that can potentially be my husband, I need to expand my horizons cuz."

"I feel you cuz, just be careful, you know as well as I do that for as long as we can both remember, females have always been jealous of you, so keep your eyes and ears open and your head on the swivel, you need to be able to spot and stop the bullshit a mile ahead."

"I appreciate you D, I really do."
"You're my little cousin, you know I gotta look out for you."

Ten minutes later I received a text message from Big Sista Squirt In Ya Face, and the message read, "*Greetings ladies, I know this is super late notice, and if you are unable to make it, we totally understand and it won't be held against you, but if you're available, tomorrow afternoon at the warehouse, we will be hosting our annual back to school drive. If you're able to make it, please come dressed in black and white. Hope to see some of you ladies tomorrow! Peace.*

"D, are you busy tomorrow afternoon?"
"Nah, why what's up?"

"I need you to keep an eye on the kids for me, I have a back to school community event to do and I need to be there."

"YOu know I got you, any time I get to spend with my little cousins it's a bonus for me, I might bring them down there, I need to see if any of your big sisters can potentially be my future wife."

"Oh, here you go, but getting them out of the house would be a good look, I'll give you gas money and money for food in case they don't eat at the event."

"DOn't insult me like that, you don't have to pay me to watch my cousins, we family, stop playin' with me."

"I appreciate you cuz, I really do."

Two Weeks later...

I received an email from the president of Delta Pi Psi which was odd because I wasn't yet in the sorority, and the email read,

"Greetings Ms. Monroe, my name is Naomi Pugh, and I am the President of Delta Pi Psi Sorority, Incorporated. I hope this email finds you well and in good health, the purpose of this email is to follow up with you about the verbal altercation between you and Soror Akria Duarte. It was brought to my attention a day or so after it happened. I apologize for taking so long to reach out to you regarding this matter. I've been trying to investigate what happened and put the pieces together so I can move forward with corrective action against Mrs. Duarte. It is my understanding that Akira is the one who initiated the verbal altercation, in front of outsiders as well as other members of your line. As you know, Delta Pi Psi Sorority has a strict policy prohibiting members and potential new members from engaging in arguments over DPP business in front of strangers. I do understand that Akira has issued a public apology, so I'm reaching out to you to see if you'd like to file a formal complaint against her before we make a final decision as to what we're going to do about her. Please feel free to email me back at your earliest convenience with your decision. Have a blessed day."

"Damn, they really take this shit seriously, I said aloud to myself before replying to Naomi's email.

"Hello Ms. Pugh, I thank you for reaching out to me regarding the incident that took place two weeks ago. As per your email, yes, Akira did apologize for her actions that morning and I have forgiven her. I do not wish to file a formal complaint, so long as Akira realizes her error and doesn't make the same mistake again. Just as I told her I've forgiven her because when I cross the burning sands, she and I will be sisters, and being a new sister coming in, I don't want any unnecessary drama between my Big Sisters and I. As far as I'm concerned, we're good with one another and for me, I can't wait to see my Big Sisters again. If you have any further questions or need more information regarding the incident, please feel free to email or call me. Be Blessed."

As soon as I sent the email, I had a text message come through.

"Good afternoon beautiful, it's Chance, we sorta met a couple of weeks back at the warehouse. I hope you remember me."

I responded via text, "Hey handsome, I sure do remember you. What took you so long to hit me up?"

"That's my bad sweetheart, it's been a hectic couple of weeks, but I'm locked in luv; how have you been?"

"I've been cool, working, chillin', waiting to see if you were going to really hit me up like you promised when you slipped your number in my pocket."

"I'm a man of my word luv, when can I take you out?"

"I'm actually free this whole week, I needed to get some things done so I took off work, what day works best for you?"

"How about tomorrow afternoon, we can have lunch or something? Where do you like to eat?"

"We can do something simple like Chili's, keep it light."

"Would you like me to pick you up or would you feel more comfortable meeting me there?"

"We can ride together, I'll text you my address right now."

"Alright sweetheart, I'll hit you up in the morning to see what time works for you for me to pick you up."

"Alright luv, sounds like a plan. Talk to you tomorrow."

Okay, so do y'all remember the shy brotha from a couple of weeks ago during my first initiation task? Well, unbeknownst to me, he slipped his name and number in my sweats pocket and somehow coaxed one of my soon to be sisters to give him my information. I was told that he had a thing for me and he'd left word with one of my soon to be sisters that he would be hitting me up within the next few days, but those few days turned into a couple of weeks, but I won't complain because he's easy on the eyes and he's got a dick the length of my arm, and thick as fuck. Anyway, I knew the attraction was there on both of our ends because the night we met, our eye contact was crazy, and the energy between us was even crazier. Just as I was about to shower and lay down for an hour or so, I received a phone call from Big Sista Porn Star.

"Hey Qortni, I hope I didn't catch you at a bad time, but I needed to talk to you real quick."

"Not a bad time at all, Trice, what's going on?"

"Not a bad time at all, what's going on?"

"I'm not sure if Mrs. Naomi Pugh has reached out to you yet or not, but if she didn't I just wanted to see where your head was at regarding the incident between you and Akira."

"She actually emailed me earlier today, I told her that I've put that incident behind me, I have no issues with Akira, her apology was enough for me and I don't want any bad energy between her and I or between any of the big sisters and I."

"Okay, cool, Akira was kind of worried about what you were going to say about the incident, but I'll let her know everything is cool on your end."

"Yeah, I'm good, I don't want or need any negative energy between myself and any of the big sisters before I cross, I'm not trying to make enemies, I'm trying to make lifelong connections."

"Cool, I'm glad my sister made the decision to let you in and had the brilliant idea to make you the Ace of your line. DO me a favor and come by the warehouse tomorrow evening around seven."

"Ok, I'll be there."

The Next Day...

At ten in the morning Chance called me to see what time worked for me for our lunch date. I knew it had to be earlier enough for us to go to lunch so I could make it back, make sure my children were straight before having to link up with the ladies. Chance picked me up around one thirty and we got to the restaurant around two, we were seated immediately .

"So, Ms. Qortni, tell me about yourself. What do you like to do with your free time? What interests you? What do you do for work?"

"Free time? I'm not sure I know what that is," I told him laughing. Then I continued, "I love everything creative, I'm a writer by design, that's been my passion since I was in elementary school. I used to keep notebooks filled with my writings, mostly my thoughts, and every time my father found them, he'd throw them away, but I haven't stopped writing since then. I love seeing my children happy too, they are my heart, and for work, I'm a phlebotomist. What about you?"

"In my free time I love spending time with my family or fraternity brothers, I love going to the movies, shooting pool or going to the arcade. I'm interested in you, seeing you a couple of weeks ago really did something to me, I've been captivated by your beauty and energy since then. For work, I'm a graphic designer and I dabble in marketing."

"Dope, what fraternity are you in?"
"Beta Delta Mu, have you heard of it?"

"I have but haven't gone in depth to find out what it's about, so enlighten me."
"Well, you know how Delta Pi Psi is an erotic sorority? Well, Beta Delta Mu is like the brother fraternity to them, we're an erotic fraternity."

"We'd make the perfect couple, both members of an erotic fraternity and sorority, it's like we were supposed to meet when we did."

"Indeed love. So, what led you to want to join an erotic sorority?"

"I love sex, I love everything about sex, from the build up conversations you and the person you're interested in have, to the foreplay once y'all get in the same space as one another, to the final act. The fact that when I see a person I'm interested in, I can damn near imagine and feel how the sex with him is going to be. The only downside to that is actually fucking him and finding out he's a total disappointment in bed, I hate having to finish myself off when there's a man in my bed next to me."

Chance started laughing then said, "We're going to get along just fine, you're a woman after my own heart shorty."

Chance and I talked for what seemed like an eternity but in reality it was only about two and a half hours. The drinks were flowing and so were my juices, if you know what I mean. I took my shoe off and began massaging his dick with my foot, and not even twenty seconds later, he was at full attention, so much so that his dick was almost hanging outside of his shorts."

"Oh you trying to start some shit in here, aren't you?"

"You already know the answer to that, don't you?" I asked him sucking the shit out of a cherry.

"You know I have something better for you to suck on, that cherry can't please you like I can."

"Oh baby, I definitely know that, you left a lasting impression on my pussy a few weeks ago."

"I can leave another lasting impression on you right now if you're down."

"Chance, come with me to the bathroom," I told him as he was leaving the payment for the bill.

"Say less," he responded, leading the way.

Thankfully the restaurant wasn't crowded and we were seated close to the bathroom.

We walked into the private bathroom and as soon as he locked the door, he grabbed me by my neck and pulled me in for one of the most passionate kisses I've ever experienced. HIs dick felt like it got harder, and I'm not sure that's even possible. While he had one hand on my neck kissing me, his other hand began undressing me from the waist down.

His free hand began finger fucking me and getting me even more wet than I already was.

"Chance, fuck me baby," I whispered to him.

"Not yet," he whispered back to me. He lifted me onto his shoulders and began eating my pussy, first kissing me on either side of my inner thighs, then his tongue started licking the inside of my pussy, when he started sucking on my clitoris, that's when the first orgasm ripped through my body, sending me into seizure like convulsions.

"That a girl, daddy has to make you cum with his tongue first before you get a taste of this dick baby."

"I want the dick now, pleaseeeeee," I said begging. DOn't judge me for begging for the dick, y'all don't understand, his dick has magical powers.

"Ask nicely for daddy's dick."
"Chance, baby, can I please have that dick rearrange my guts again? Please and thank you in advance?"

"That's better," he responded before taking his monster dick out of his pants, putting a BDM XXL condom on and gently lowering me onto him.

"Ohmyfuckinggawd!!!!" I said in his ear as another orgasm ripped through my body like a bolt of lightning.

"You shaking already and I haven't even done anything yet, you good?" He asked with a smirk on his face.

"I'm better than good."
With each stroke my body became weaker and weaker, I was silently praying that my meeting

with the ladies later this evening didn't entail me fucking or sucking anything because I knew my performance would be subpar, Chance was depleting my energy but I wasn't complaining in the least bit.

After thirty minutes of him rearranging my insides, we climaxed together and I promise I felt like his condom broke as he was coming, I just hoped I wasn't ovulating. I looked at my watch and noticed that I didn't have too much time to get home, shower and get dressed before my meeting with the ladies later this evening.

"Chance, I hate to cut this date short but I have a meeting I need to be at this evening and I need to get home to shower and get ready for it."

"No worries love, I have to go out this evening as well. Hopefully either later this week or next week we can link up again, maybe go bowling or shoot pool or something, if you're up to it."

"That sounds like a plan, after tonight I should know what my schedule is like for the rest of this week or next week."

Chance dropped me off at home, I had enough time to shower and get an hour nap before I needed to begin getting ready for this meeting. At six o'clock, I started getting ready to meet the ladies at the warehouse. I had no idea what this meeting was about or what it was going to entail. I wasn't sure what to put on so I kept it cute and classy. I put on a cute pair of jeans, a fitted t-shirt and a pair of silver stilettos.

When I got to the warehouse I saw Chance's car parked in the parking lot, I said aloud to myself, "What the fuck is going on?"

When Chance saw me walk through the doors and greet the sisters, he subtly shook his head as if to tell me not to greet him, so I obliged.

Laniyah was standing next to an older woman whom I'd never seen before so I was really thrown off and had no idea as to what was going on.

"Qortni, it's so nice to meet you in person, I've heard nothing but good things about you, I'm Naomi Pugh."

"Oh wow, so nice to meet you in person Mrs. Pugh."

"The pleasure is all mine. These lovely ladies have been singing your praises since your first meeting, and now I see why. Can I just say how stunningly beautiful you are?"

"Wow, thank you for the compliment. I'm sorry, I'm a little lost, I'm not sure what's going on here right now, am I in some type of trouble? Was I told to come here so you can tell me in person that I'm getting kicked off the line?"

"Oh gracious no, nothing like that, we would never do a thing like that to anyone, we'd never play in anyone's face like that. The purpose of me having your Big Sisters have you here this evening is so you can complete your initiation task tonight. From what they've been telling me and from the way you handled yourself with the altercation with Akira, and how you were adamant about not wanting any bad energy or animosity between you and your big sisters, you are the prime example of what Delta Pi Psi Sorority, Incorporated embodies. You are here tonight to complete your initiation, and your last initiation task is with a one on one session with my nephew, Chance Pugh. The two of you will have thirty minutes, Qortni, you will have thirty minutes to make him tap out, there are no restrictions on the sexual acts you can do to make it happen. Once your thirty minutes are up, there will be two knocks at the door, the both of you must then come out how you are, naked and all. You will be being watched as we have a camera set up in the room. Are you ready?"

I took a deep breath, thought about this last initiation task, looked Naomi in her eyes and said, "I was born for this." Then I looked at Chance and said, "I'm ready when you are handsome."

Chance and I walked to the back room in complete silence, we didn't want our cover blown with his aunt and my soon to be sorority sister. As soon as we got to the room, his dick was rock hard, I smirked and winked at him, I guess our rendezvous earlier on our date was still fresh in his mind, cause it was damn sure still fresh in mine and my pussy was still trying to recover from it, she'd been stretched out quite a bit.

I walked over and sat on the bed, slowly unbuttoned my pants, and pulled them down to my ankles, then I started playin' with my pussy and asshole at the same time. Our eyes locked and he began slowly stroking his already erect dick and licking his lips like he was Uncle LL or some shit!

"You know you're not going to make me tap out, right?"

"Oh baby, I will and I'm going to have fun doing it too, cause you're about to stuff all of that dick of yours into this tight asshole of mine, you're not going to last more than ten minutes in it, guaranteed."

"Oh, so that's how you want to play?"

"You came in here talking big shit so now you have to pay."

Chance put a BDM XXL condom on, walked over to me still stroking his big ass dick. "Bring that dick here and stuff me like a piñata," I told him while lubing my ass up.

"Be careful what you ask for," he whispered in my ear."

I whispered back, "I only ask for what I want, nothing more, never less. Now get ready to tap out in five minutes."

I arched my back and got ready to take Chance on the ride of his life.
"FUCK!!" He yelled as he felt how tight my asshole was.

"I told you," I said, smirking at him.
Not even ten strokes in yet and Chance tapped out, I laughed and said, "I knew it was only a matter of time."

"Yo, you are something else," he said laughing as well.
We both got dressed, and returned to the main part of the warehouse where all of the other sisters were as well as Naomi.

To my surprise, all of the sisters were dressed in white and had somehow decorated the main warehouse in the sorority colors.

"Qortni, come please," Naomi said, then she added, "Chance, thank you, I'll talk to you later, but for now, you are dismissed."

Laniyah then said, "Qortni, you pulled it off, every test we've put you through, whether it was here or anywhere else, you passed."

My face must not have been using her inside voice because Trice started laughing at the fact that I was totally oblivious to what Laniyah meant when she said that they tested me without my knowledge.

"Your outing today with Chance, that was partially our doing, as a member of Delta Pi Psi Sorority, Incorporated, you have to be willing to get down, dirty and freaky at a moments notice and you passed that test with flying colors from what we were told," Trice told me.

"Oh shit," I responded laughing, then added, "well played."

"We know, some of the other sisters whom I hadn't yet had the opportunity to meet yet, said at the same time."

"Qortni, I'm sorry, I mean, Ms. Alluring Tigress, you have exemplified the qualities of a true leader, you are a beautiful young lady and from what we've seen, you are a woman who owns her sexuality and who isn't afraid to be uninhibited. It is with great pleasure to pin you and welcome you as the newest member of Delta Pi Psi SOrority, Incorporated," Naomi stated.

I began crying, like really boo-hoo crying because if you know what I've been through, then you'd know what this accomplishment means to me.

Naomi pinned me, then in walked Chance, my two children, and my cousin Derrell.

"Congratulations cuz!! I'm super proud of you!"

"D!! Thank you so much!!

"Mommy, congratulations on your big accomplishment!" my son said to me, hugging me.

"Ladies, I think Qortni deserves for us to take her and her family out to eat tonight at the restaurant of her choosing, so where will it be Qornti?"

"Let's go to Olive Garden."
"Olive Garden it is, we will all meet up at Olive Garden in North Haven. I'll call and make the reservations, it's twenty of us, correct?" Laniyah stated.

When we got to the restaurant, Chance sat to the right of me and my children sat in between Derrell and myself.

"So beautiful, I hope you don't look at me any differently for not telling you that I was brought in to be a part of your initiation."

"Not at all love, I have enjoyed every moment we've spent together."

"Well, how about we continue spending time together and see if we can turn this into something permanent?"

"I think I'd like that. I'm lying, I know I'd like that."

"Great, and I hope you don't think that my aunt is going to have any say so in our relationship now that you're a member of the sorority."

"Sweetheart, we're grown, there's no one that can tell me whether or not I can be in a relationship with you. I know how to separate personal from professional."

"My girl," he said, smiling before kissing me on the forehead.

We all ate, talked and I got to meet all of my new big sisters, I was a little taken aback that Akira wasn't in attendance but I wasn't going to question what happened to her, it was out of my pay grade and I was enjoying the fact that one of my lifelong dreams had finally come true! I was now a part of a sisterhood, something I've always felt was missing from my life, having a sister, now I have a lot of them.

I hope you have enjoyed but best believe this is nowhere near the end of my story...there's more to cum, a lot more....

Qortni Monore

a.k.a.
Alluring Tigress

BONUS READ!!!!!

My Holiday Love

It was a few weeks away from Christmas, I was stressed as hell trying to pull off my first Christmas without my village, my father was gone and now, my favorite aunt, this was going to be a different type of Christmas for my children and I.

Right after I dropped my children off and before I went to work, I headed to Walmart to find some inexpensive decorations so I could at least fake the funk this holiday season for my children. They each had their own trees, but the ornaments needed some upgrades, and I wanted to decorate the front of our house, something that we never did before.

I was on my way to see my client in Wallingford, it was cold and there was a bit of snow on the ground. He was my second to last client for the day, so I was extremely happy that my work day was about to be over. When I arrived at my client's office, I called to let him know I was a little early, but I was there.

"Hello Mr. Hollis, I'm just letting you know that I'm early but I am at your office." "Cool, I 'm running late but I'll be there shortly."

"You have about five minutes to get here before I leave and you'll have to reschedule." "Bet."

As I sat in his office waiting room, there were a bunch of Christmas decorations, which made me want to leave quickly. I really wasn't in the holiday spirit. Sitting in his office, I realized we had something in common, we were both into real estate, I was an investor and he was a realtor. When he walked into his office, he greeted his secretary and told me to follow him. When we got to his office, he sat with his back to me, on his laptop as I began his exam. When he finally turned towards me to answer a question, it was at that moment I was able to see his face, and damn if this man wasn't foine.

"Damn," I mistakenly said aloud.

"Something wrong?"

"Not at all, everything is all good." We finished the questionnaire portion of his exam and it was time for me to get his measurements. I did his chest measurements and that's when I realized he smelled as good as he looked, I really wanted to suck his dick right there and then, but I had to remain professional.

Scenarios of him fuckin' me on his table in his office began to play in my mind, him laying me on the table, tearing my clothes off and sliding his already hard dick into my throbbing pussy, making me cum over and over again. I envisioned him putting me on all fours and digging me out from the back while one of his hands began to play with my clit and one of my hands massaged his balls as he brought me to ecstasy. I snapped back to reality when his office door closed and he came back in handing me his urine specimen.

We wrapped up his appointment and I was on my way to my last clients. I then got a text message that read, "*Hello Bria, this is Dylan, you just completed my insurance exam.*"

I text back, "*Hey, did I leave something at your office?*"

"*No, nothing like that, I don't normally do this but I wanted to say that I think you're beautiful and I love your vibe. Do you mind if I keep your number?*"

I started dancing in my car, I knew the vibe between us I was feeling wasn't off. I then responded back, "*I don't mind at all.*"

He told me to text him after I finished with my last clients, and I promised to do so.

Later that evening...

"*Can you talk now?*"

"*Sure.*"

Dylan called me, "Hey beautiful, how did the rest of your day go?"

"It was pretty chill, I picked my babies up from school, cooked dinner, now I'm working on one of my books."

"Wait, you're a writer?"
"Yeah, I have three books out so far."

"Dope, what kind of books do you write?"
"Fiction, the three I have out so far are on domestic violence, mainly my life in fiction."

"Damn, I 'm sorry you had to endure that. I don't read those types of books but I'd definitely like to support you. I'll give the book to my mother, she loves to read."

"Nice, send me your mailing address and I'll send it out tomorrow and I'll send you my cash app and you can pay me for it."

"What are your plans tomorrow afternoon around three-thirty?"
"After I pick my children up, I'm good, what did you have in mind?"

"*I would love to see you, how about we meet up in Hamden, that way I can get the book from you instead of you shipping it.*"

"*Sounds like a plan.*"

We talked a little more before hanging up, then we started texting each other for the next three hours.

Three Weeks Later

"*Bria, are you busy this evening?*" Read the text I received from Dylan.

"*Not really, why, what's up?*"

"*I want to invite you over, I haven't been able to get you out of my mind since we sat and had drinks a few weeks ago.*"

"*Let me get my kids dinner cooked and get them squared away, shower and I'll let you know when I'm on my way. Text me over your address,*" I replied to his text.

Once I got my kids dinner cooked, they ate, I bathed them, then took my shower and let my younger brother know I was on my way out, he told me he'd keep an eye on my children for me.

I made my way to Dylan's house which was about a thirty minute drive from me, when I got out of the car, I was rudely reminded of how cold it was and how underdressed I was, as I only had on a t-shirt dress and a pair of ankle boots, and when I said that's all I had on, that's exactly what I mean. I sent him a text that I was here so he could let me into the building.

Once we got into his apartment, I straddled him as soon as he sat next to me. Everything I had imagined in my head while in his office the day we met was about to come true if I had anything to do with it. I began kissing his neck, and I could feel his dick getting harder by the second.

"Bria hold up," he told me as he lifted me up and placed me on the couch next to him. "Is something wrong?"

'Nah, nothing is wrong," he said as he was adjusting himself. "I just want to slow things down a little bit," he said looking directly into my eyes.

"Oh, um, ok, cool."

"Trust me, had we met like a year or two ago, I'd be all over you but there's something about you that intrigues me and I want to get to know you a little better before getting in between your knees."

Now why'd he go and say that shit? That made me hornier and wetter, I crossed my legs and we began to talk, get to know one another more and before we knew it, it was already one in the morning and I had to be on the road headed south in the next five hours. He walked me to my car, surprisingly kissed me passionately and I made my way home.

Two weeks later

"So Bria, I have something to admit to you and I really don't want to admit it, but I miss you, and I want to see if you're open to spending the holidays with my family and I?"

"Is this an invitation for my children as well? Or just for me?"

"Of course your children are invited, but I also want to meet them without my family being around, so are the three of you available this Saturday afternoon? Maybe we can have lunch or something. What's their favorite restaurant?

"We are available Saturday, we don't have to go out to eat, we can do something else, but it's totally up to you."

"See what they may want to do and let me know, I want to meet them in a comfortable environment."

"You're the only man I've dealt with that has asked to meet my children, this makes me kinda like you even more."

Quiet as it's kept, I was falling hard for Dylan, like Alicia Keys type *Fallin'* for this man, and what made it even better was that he wanted to meet my children. My babies were top priority in my life, so knowing that I was dealing with someone who saw that and wanted to be a part of that was top tier to me.

We decided on lunch, which didn't surprise me because my children had healthy appetites like I did. We met Dylan at Chili's in Wallingford, cause it didn't make sense to me to have him drive all the way to East Haven or Milford. The holiday traffic was beginning to irritate me, what would normally be a twenty minute drive took almost an hour because of ignorant drivers. The conversations between my children and Dylan were heartwarming, he was the first man they've seen me interact with on any level other than their father. Later that evening, Dylan and I met up for drinks.

"How did your kids like hanging out with me earlier?"

"They loved it and for some reason, they really like you."

"What do you mean for some reason? I'm great with children, and your children are great, you've done well by them."

"Thank you for the compliment, but it's nothing, I'm just being the best mother I can be to my babies, that's all, it's nothing special."

"Nah, it's definitely something special, you're someone special and so are your children, so the invitation is still open for the three of you to join my family and I for the holidays, if you'd like."

"Absolutely, my children told me on the way home earlier that they wanted to see you again, so spending the holidays with you will make them very happy."

"Cool, I've told my mother and sisters about you already and they're looking forward to meeting you and your children."

"Nice, well, I know you've spent most of your day with me, and I'm not trying to wear out my welcome with you, so I'm going to call it an evening."

"I can never get tired of being around you and I was hoping we'd go back to my place and chill a little while longer, but if you need to go, I understand."

"Lead the way sir."

As soon as we got into his apartment, we were all over each other, clothes flying everywhere, he lifted me up and brought me to his bedroom and laid me on the bed. He grabbed a condom out of his top drawer and put it on, when he entered me, I could do nothing but gasp, he felt like heaven inside of me.

"Damn," was all Dylan could manage to say.

We locked eyes as we were in the missionary position, this was no ordinary fuck session, we both knew what it was but I think we both may have been thinking the same thing, it was way too early to utter that L word.

"Dylan, you feel too damn good inside of me, fuck!"

"You got me wanting to take this condom off."

I couldn't help but laugh, I wanted to warn him but I decided against it, cause I knew that if he took that condom off, tonight would be the absolute last time he'd ever put one on. An hour and a half later, we climaxed together, well, his first orgasm and my tenth. Dylan had definitely earned the number one spot in my book when we came to my sexual partners.

Christmas Eve

From the first night Dylan and I made love it seemed as if we grew closer together, we talked more during the day and night, we'd FaceTime one another and be on until three or four in the morning, which was shame on me because I knew I had to be up by six in the morning.

On this particular Christmas Eve evening, my children and I met Dylan at his place and we all rode to his parents house together, and to say I was nervous was an understatement, I had butterflies and the bubble guts all in one.

Dylan was absolutely amazing and so patient with my children, this man had me envisioning the four of us really being a family and my children having the positive male role model they so desperately needed. As we were getting ready to leave, he pulled me into one of the back bedrooms, he said he had something to ask me.

"Bria, I know we've known one another for only a short period of time, but I promise you these feelings I have for you are real, and no matter how hard I try to shake them, they won't go anywhere," then it happened, he got on one knee, then said, "Bria, I'm in love with you and my life won't be complete unless you and the children are apart of it, so I'm asking you if you would do me the honor of being my wife?"

"Hell yes!" I screamed loudly, with tears freely falling down my face.

My children ran into the room to see what was going on, then my son said, "it's about time! We get to have a real father now!"

As soon as our engagement was confirmed, out of nowhere Dylan's youngest sister began playing one of my favorite songs, 'He Proposed' by Kelly Price.

Dylan and the children wanted to go out to eat to celebrate our new engagement, so we were lucky to get a table at Wood-n-Tap, we ordered a bunch of appetizers and I just basked in the reality that my dream for the past year was coming true, my forever love had come into my life at the most difficult time in my life and helped me do a complete 180. Once we left the restaurant, it was super late and Dylan didn't want me driving back home so all of us stayed at his house for the night, and to my surprise, when we got there, he had a huge Christmas tree in his living room with gifts wrapped with my children's names on them, he was truly a man full of surprises tonight.

Tears began to freely fall as I looked around his house, we put the kids in his bed and we settled on the couch.

"When did you do all of this?! The last time I was here none of this was here."

"I'd been shopping for your children for a while now, I wanted them to have a great Christmas because I knew they were probably going to be thinking about your father and aunt this year, so I wanted to lighten your burden a little and do something for y'all. I hope I haven't overstepped?"

"No you haven't overstepped, this is the nicest thing anyone has ever done for my children and I. I swear I love you so much," I told him sobbing.

He began wiping the tears from my face, then embraced me. I felt so safe and secure in his arms, I hope this feeling never ends. I kissed him passionately before straddling him, his actions were definitely deserving of more than a verbal thank you from me. With each kiss, his dick grew, poking me constantly; he picked me up and laid me on the couch, we had to make sure we were as quiet as can be so we didn't wake the kids. He began to plant small kisses all over my body, pulling my t-shirt dress over my head, he stopped and just stared at me, 'damn you're fine," was all he said. He cupped each of my breasts as his tongue made its way to my love section. The moment his tongue touched my clit, I knew it was going to be hard for me to keep the noise down, cause when the dick and mouth are good, I get loud.

We moved the party from the couch to the floor. I wasn't about to let Dylan outdo me in the oral department, so we changed positions so we could do 69, and if I do say so myself, I definitely put it down on him. He tapped me twice on my ass, I knew that meant it was time for me to let up off of him and that he was about to put it down on me, so we changed positions again. I laid on the floor, and he entered me, and my legs immediately began to shake. He knew how to make my body and I feel good.

"I haven't done anything yet and here you go with ya legs shakin'," he said laughing.

"Yo, shut up! You always say you don't be doin' anything when you be doin' a whole lot, and you know you do!"

Dylan's thrusts and mine were in sync, we were locked in with one another, not taking our eyes off one another. In my opinion, that's the best type of love making, missionary, eyes locked in and just enjoying one another. We climaxed together, then showered together and ended our night with Dylan putting The Best Man Holiday on and we fell asleep with him holding me.

Christmas Day

My children woke up around five in the morning, of course waking Dylan and I up to ask if they could open their gifts, and of course, Dylan obliged. While Dylan busied himself with the kids, I showered and began making breakfast. Halfway into making breakfast, I felt dizzy and the next thing I remembered was waking up on the couch to my children crying.

"Bria, Bria, can you hear me?" Dylan asked, obviously worried.

"Yea, I can hear you, what happened?"
"You passed out in the kitchen, we're about to take you to the hospital."

"I'm not going to the hospital, it's Christmas Day and it's going to be packed in there. I feel fine."
"You are so stubborn and hardheaded."
"I know, which is one of the reasons you love me so much."
"Listen, take it easy today, if you pass out again or even look like you're not feeling well, you're

going to the hospital, and I'm not taking no for an answer."

"Fine Dylan, now can we continue enjoying Christmas? Kids, we have to get our things together, you have more gifts to open at the house."

"Dylan, are you coming with us to our house?" My daughter Paige asked.

"If it's alright with your mother, I would love to come."
"You're driving, of course it's alright with me," I replied laughing.

Three Days Later
Dylan and I were in the shower together, my children were at my half-sister's house with their cousins, so Dylan and I had a few hours to enjoy one another uninterrupted. I was on my knees giving Dylan some oral romance because quite honestly, it's my favorite part of sex. As I was getting up so I could position myself so

Dylan could enter me from behind, I got dizzy again and almost passed out.

"Bria, we're going to the hospital, I'm not taking no for an answer, let me get your clothes and help you get dressed."

"Fine, I'm not even in the mood to argue with you," I told him while checking my pulse. My heart was racing and I didn't know what the cause was, and for me to have passed out a few days ago and on the verge of passing out again not too long ago, I needed to find out what was going on with me, I was starting to get a little scared.

"Bae, when did all of this passing out stuff begin?"

"Christmas morning, why?"

"When was your last period?"

"I have to check my phone, I don't think I've missed a period though."

"You know you can still get your period and be pregnant, right?"

"I know, remember I told you that happened to me when I was pregnant with my daughter, I just feel like I've managed to stay away from you while I'm ovulating."

"Wait, you really do that?"

"I know how fertile I am and I also know that we've stopped using condoms a while ago, so hell yea I do that," I told him laughing.

When we got to the hospital, my blood pressure was extremely low, so they took me to a room immediately. "Bria, when was the first day of your last period?" My nurse asked me.

I unlocked my phone, went to my calendar and realized I had missed my period; "Apparently, I've seemed to have missed my period a few days ago, but isn't that too soon to tell if I'm pregnant?"

"Not necessarily, but we're going to do two different tests, we're going to have you leave a urine sample to do a regular pregnancy test, then we're going to do blood work, which is more precise to determine whether or not you are pregnant."

"Thank you," Dylan said to the nurse. Tears began to fall freely down my face.
"Are you alright? Are you still feeling dizzy?"

"I'm good, it's just a whole lot happening in such a short time, but I'm good, thanks."
"If you need anything, just push the red button on your remote and I'll be in."

"Thank you so much DeNae, we appreciate you."
"Are you nervous about the possibility of us being pregnant?"

"Truthfully, yes I am, I mean, this is all going pretty fast, you're not nervous?"
"No, because I have the woman of my dreams possibly carrying our first child together, I get to be a bonus father to Paige and Peyton, I'm winning in every aspect of life right now."

"You are too good to be true, I swear I love you, and I know with you by my side, we're going to be just fine."

"Babe, I know since we've met and the many discussions we've had you always expressed not having a wedding, but instead going to the Justice of the Peace, what do you think about getting married on New Year's Eve?"

"That's a few days away, you sure?"
"I'm just as sure as I was the night I made the decision that you were the woman for me, and the night I proposed to you."

"I'm here for it my love, you lead and I'll follow."
"That's my girl, do I need to grab the kids from your sister's house? Oh, and what about..." Before Dylan was able to finish his statement, my nurse, DeNae, came back in.

"How are we feeling?"

"Starting to feel better, did you come in here to do my bloodwork?"

"Indeed I did, as well as to see if you feel well enough to possibly leave us a urine sample; has the doctor been in to see you yet?"

"No, you're the only one that's been in, and I think I can manage to leave a sample, I've been holding my pee for the past twenty minutes," I told her sitting up to get my bearings straight.

"Take your time, the bathroom is literally about five feet from your room, and when you come back in, we'll do your bloodwork, unless you want to do that first."

"Yea, we can do that first, then I'll go to the bathroom, because I'm going to assume that I'm going to get at least one more saline bag before I get discharged."

"You must've been through this before," DaNae said laughing.

"Twice already but this time is definitely better because I have my love here with me," I said winking at Dylan.

In such a short period of time he came into my life and literally turned it around for the better; just when I was starting to give up on love because of all of the failed situationships and failed relationships I had to deal with, he came in, approached me in a manner in which I wasn't used to and, made me a believer in authentic love, and knight in shining armors.

"How long have y'all been married?"

"We're actually getting married on New Year's Eve."

"Oh 'Em GEE! I love holiday weddings, well congratulations to the both of you. The way you are with one another, it seems as if you've been together for a long time. Bria, you're going to feel a little poke as the needle is going in, it's only one tub being drawn, so this will be a very quick process."

"I know, I'm a phlebotomist, so I know the process," I told DeNae as I closed my eyes. Then I said to Dylan, "babe, grab an emesis bag for me please."

As soon as the bag made it to my hand, everything I'd eaten earlier came back up, I was really starting to believe I was pregnant.

"DeNae, how soon will the bloodwork results come back?"

"If the lab isn't busy, they should be back in about an hour or so, if not, you'll definitely have them by tomorrow, but we're also doing a regular urine pregnancy test too, and they are about ninety-seven percent accurate."

"Great; I know her previous two successful pregnancies she had to have an IV drip at home and a visiting nurse because she gets really sick, so I just want to get ahead of this before it gets any worse for her, so I apologize if I'm asking too many questions or if it seems as if I'm overstepping."

"You're good, I understand you're concerned about your fiancé, you're not being a bother to me, no need to apologize."
Just as DeNae was done with my bloodwork, Dylan helped me to the bathroom so I could leave a urine sample.

Two Days Later

"Babe, I just got the notification on my phone that my bloodwork results just came in."

"What do they say?" Dylan asked while handing me a cup of peppermint and ginger tea.

"We're about to expand our family," I said in a faint voice.

"Are you happy about it or still worried that this is still moving fast?"
"I'm good with the results, I'll be even better when this twenty-four seven sickness is over."

"Hopefully once the first trimester is over with, it'll subside, but until then, anything you need, I'm here for you."

"How are you going to be there for me when we live in two different houses?"

"That's something we're going to need to discuss, I know we're both settled into our respective homes, but now that we'll be getting married within the next forty-eight hours, what are your thoughts on our living situation going forward?"

"I think we're going to need a bigger space, especially with the baby on the way."

"So, are we getting a bigger place or am I moving into your house for now?"
"What are your thoughts on the situation?"

"I'm comfortable with moving into your spot for now, that way we can continue to save and get our own spot within the next year or so, I think that makes the most sense."

"I'm not going to dispute you on that, I think it makes the most sense as well, but there is something else that we need to discuss, and that's whether or not we plan on staying here in Connecticut. You know when we first met I put it out there that Connecticut was not going to be my residence for too much longer, so when we do buy this new house next year, is it going to be in Connecticut?"

"That's going to be a conversation we're going to have to have, something that won't be agreed upon overnight."

"Dylan, you can do your real estate anywhere, I'm sure the company you're with will have no issues with you transferring. Both of my jobs are transferable and to be quite honest with you, everything I'm doing business wise it makes more sense for me to be down south."

"I'm not negating anything you're saying, and i know we've had this discussion when we first met, you were adamant about not staying here, but you also have to realize I've been helping to take care of my mother and younger sisters, and I don't want them to feel a type of way if I were to just up and move down south."

"It's all sounding like an excuse to me, but you do what you feel is best for you and I'm going to do the same."

"Bria, don't be like that, I'm just trying to communicate with you and tell you how I truly feel, I never said moving was out of the question for me, I just feel like a year is really fast, so all I'm saying is that this is a conversation that's going to take a little while to sort out and come to a mutual agreement about."

"Fine Dylan, if that's the case, then maybe getting married tomorrow isn't the best thing for us, how about we postpone it," I told him, obviously upset.

"Are you sure? We can talk this through tonight and still be good for tomorrow."

"As of this moment, we can postpone the wedding. I feel like my feelings are being dismissed and I don't like or appreciate that, so as of right now, I'm good on getting married tomorrow."

"FIne, I'll be back tomorrow morning to see how you're feeling and to check on you and the kids."

"Bye," I replied, rolling my eyes.
I needed time to really think about all of this. DId I love Dylan? Without question but I wasn't willing to push my feelings to the side to accommodate him and his feelings, and I didn't appreciate the fact that he knew coming into my world that I wasn't planning on staying in Connecticut, so i'm beginning to wonder if him getting me pregnant was done purposely just to keep me here until he decided he was ready to leave.

New Year's Eve

I hadn't been able to sleep, my thoughts were all over the place and if i'm being honest with myself, I was missing Dylan something serious. I knew his intentions with me were pure from the jump, and after thinking and talking to one of my favorite people, I realized that while we both had a difference of opinion when it came to relocating, I may have overreacted. I was about ninety-eight percent sure that I still wanted to marry Dylan today, I just hoped that our disagreement didn't scare him away.

Just as I was getting out of the shower and beginning to make breakfast for the kids and I, my doorbell rang and to my surprise, it was Dylan, not certain why he didn't use his key.

"Hey love, how are you feeling today?"
"I'm good, how are you?"

"Sleepy, wasn't able to sleep much last night."

"Me either, our disagreement hasn't been sitting too well with me. I started to call you last night but I wasn't sure if you'd answer or not, so I just didn't bother."

"I definitely would have answered your call, you should know that by now, no matter what disagreement we have if you call, I'm going to always answer."

"I appreciate you saying that, and I want to apologize for not completely hearing you out last night and allowing my feelings to get the best of me."

"No need to apologize, I know all of this is pretty sudden and I know it seemed as if I wasn't taking your feelings into consideration about the whole moving situation, and I never want you to feel like that again, I was being a little selfish about not wanting to move in a year, we can definitely visit this conversation again. I really wanted to come over to apologize and to check on you and the children."

"Dylan, I love you and from today on, I promise not to let another night go by when we have a disagreement to let the sun set with us upset with one another, it didn't sit right with my spirit."

"And I promise to you today that there will never be another day or night when we have a disagreement that I will rest my head before making it right with you and making sure we are good."

"So Mr. Hollis, are we jumping the broom today or nah?"
"The choice is yours Ms. Bacote, the ball for today's fate is in your court."

"Well then, let's get the kids ready so we can be the Hollis Family, party of four and a half for the new year!"

"So, instead of going to the Justice of the Peace, I rearranged some things and I actually have a minister coming here. I figured it would be easier for you, just in case you started feeling ill or anything, you'd be at home."

"What did I do to deserve someone as thoughtful as you?"

"I don't know but I know you're a very blessed woman," he responded, winking at me.

"You get on my nerves."

Dylan started helping my son get his clothes ready and got him in the shower as my daughter went to the second bathroom to take her shower and get dressed. While the children were getting ready, I decided to grab a quick nap to make sure I was good, thankfully the natural remedies I've been using to help this nausea subside had been working great.

An hour later I woke up to Dylan and the children looking so good dressed in all white and do y'all know what my man did for me? My man, Mr. Dylan Hollis bought me a brand new white outfit just for the wedding, and he knows me so well because he got me a white pants jumpsuit and some brand new white Air Force 1's to go with it, cause I damn sure wasn't about to be wearing heels. As I was getting dressed I heard Dylan's parents and sisters come in, and right after that, the minister came in.

Because neither one of us were too traditional, there wasn't regular wedding music playing in the house, as I was walking into the family room, Spend My Life With You by Eric Benet and Tamia began playing, and the waterworks began for Dylan and myself, he was standing near the minister and I think as soon as he saw me he started crying and when I saw him and my children standing there, I began crying, a whole hot mess I was.

Good afternoon. Dylan, Bria and I would like to welcome everyone on this gorgeous day. It's because of all of you, because of this strong community, Dylan and Bria's relationship has strengthened and grown and led them to this very moment. Thank you for being here, now let's begin.

"Do you, Dylan Lamar Hollis take Bria LeNae Bacote to be your lawfully wedded wife, to have and to hold from this day forward, for better and worse, in sickness and health, to love, cherish and honor her, for as long as you both shall live?" the minister asked.

"I do until my last breath."

"Do you, Bria LeNae Bacote take Dylan Lamar Hollis to be your lawfully wedded husband, to have and to hold from this day forward, for better and worse, in sickness and health, to love, cherish and honor him, for as long as you both shall live?" the minister asked me.

"I do a million times over."

"Dylan and Bria, bear witness to the love of God in this world, so that those to whom love is a stranger will find in you good and generous friends. By the power vested in me by God and man, I pronounce you husband and wife. What

God has joined together, let no man put asunder. You may now kiss the bride."

Dylan and I embraced in a kiss that reminded me of the very first time he surprised me and kissed me the first evening he invited me over to his house.

"Should we make the announcement now? Or should we wait?"

"If you want to make it now, go ahead my love."

"So, being that our loved ones are here, we have an announcement to make, between late August and early September, we will be welcoming a new baby into the family!"

My children looked at each other, then ran to Dylan and I and embraced us, then my son, Peyton said, "I get to be a big brother now?"

"You sure do! Are you happy you're no longer the little brother?"

"Yes! Now I'll have someone to boss around!"

Everyone laughed, then the minister said, "I think now it's an appropriate time to say a prayer over your family, there is nothing more precious than bringing new life into the world, so let's all bow our heads and close our eyes in prayer. Dear Heavenly Father, we come to you today because in your word You said that if two or more shall agree on earth there you are in the midst of them, so with more than two of us gathered here today, we touch and agree that Dylan, Bria, Paige and Peyton will be able to welcome a healthy baby into their family towards the end of the upcoming year. Lord we thank you in advance that Bria will have a smooth pregnancy and an even smoother delivery, in Christ Jesus name we pray, and everyone in agreement, says, "Amen."

Everyone said 'Amen' in unison. After that prayer, I began to feel better about the pregnancy and truth be told, the nausea I was beginning to experience started to dissipate.

With every pregnancy, I've always felt as if I were going to miscarry because I dealt with severe hyperemesis, but my nerves were calmed and my spirit was uplifted, and that was all thanks to Dylan and the minister he chose for us today.

After the ceremony and prayer, we all went out to grab some soul food. There was no way I was cooking tonight, so we made sure we ordered enough to bring back to the house with us for later in the evening and tomorrow.

Mid February

The pregnancy has been going great, I also think the sex between Dylan and I has been great, they always say pregnant sex is better, but not to toot my own horn, but I've never had a complaint from any partners in the sex department. The children were about to be out of school for their winter break, so Dylan and I decided to take a family trip to Georgia for the week. I was still cautious and taking it easy until the end of my first trimester; I know Dylan loves and treats my children as his own but there's nothing like being able to give the man you love a child of his own that shares his DNA.

After getting off of the plane, we grabbed our luggage and went straight to the hotel. I was tired and jetlagged. When we got to the rooms, Dylan got the kids set up in their room, which was adjoined to our room, and the best part was that one of Dylan's sisters accompanied us to help out with the children.

"Babe, would you rather get room service or go out to eat tonight?"

"We can go out, I'm sure the children and your sister want to get out of the room cause what's a vacation if we stay in the room?"

"Say less, let me see where the kids want to eat, don't get in the shower til I get back please and thank you."

"Listen, you're trying to make us stay in and have to order room service, remember, we got one on the way already."

"We sure do and if I have my way, Imma knock another one in you and they'll be in there together for a lil while."

"You're crazy, hurry up and see where the kids want to eat so we can shower please."

As Dylan was in the adjoining room trying to help the children figure out where we were going to eat, I started the shower. Just as I stepped in, Dylan came in behind me.

"I thought I told you to wait for me, you don't listen," he told me, slapping my ass.

"You know I'm hard headed, I think I need to be disciplined and taught a lesson," I told him seductively.

"You better believe I'm going to teach you a lesson," he told me, grabbing my neck from behind and kissing my back.

I turned to face him, got down in a squatting position and started sucking his dick.

"Fuck," he said in a faint voice.

"You like that, don't you? You love the way my lips feel on your dick, don't you?

"Fuck Bria, you know I do. Stand up baby, let me show you just how much I love it."

He helped me up, put one of my legs on the side of the tub, then he got on his knees and began to eat my pussy.

"Dylan, baby, this feels so damn good, oh my goodness," I told him with one of my hands on his head.

"How good does it feel?"

"Damn good, fuck, I'm about to cum baby."

"Cum all over daddy's tongue, let me taste it all baby."

My legs began to shake and the rest of my body began to shake as well.

Dylan stood up, picked me up and entered me, and dammit if he didn't feel good being inside of me.

We decided to move this party to the bed so we didn't bust our asses in the shower, and because I knew Dylan wanted to be able to get all in my guts and being in the shower would have prohibited him from doing so.

"You locked our door didn't you? Don't want the kids or your sister just walking in on us."

"Yea, I got us covered, you just worry about enjoying all this dick I'm about to bless you with."

"I'm ready baby."

We were in the missionary position, eyes locked in and in sync, then Dylan did something totally unexpected and new. As we were making love, he slipped one of his fingers into my ass, and that made my next orgasm much more powerful.

This anal play was something I could get used to, I made a mental note to have Dylan and I stop by an adult store after we got the kids back to the hotel to grab some anal lube, he now had me wanting to try anal sex.

We got up, showered quickly, got dressed and went out to eat, then we went sightseeing. This was the first time I was in Atlanta for pleasure and nothing business related. The children especially loved going to the Georgia Aquarium. We got through maybe half of it before the children started getting tired, so we left and dropped them and my sister-in-law off before going to one of the adult stores.

"Tell me again why we're going to this adult store?"

"I want to get some anal lube, our session earlier has me wanting to try anal sex now."

"Oh really? What brought that on?" he asked with a devilish grin.

"You slipping your finger into my asshole while we were making love brought that on, but you knew that already."

"I did my love, I absolutely did. Have you ever thought about bringing toys into the bedroom with us?"

"No, but that's only because I'm not sure how much I'd be able to take, you already take my body to higher heights when we make love, bringing toys into the mix will probably make me have convulsions, I don't know if I'm ready for all of that."

He shook his head and began laughing because he knew what I was saying was the honest to God truth. We purchased a few pornos and a few tubes of anal lube because I was certain I'd love anal sex and I didn't want to run out anytime soon.

On the way back to the hotel I surprised Dylan by giving him head while he drove back to the hotel.

"Oh, so this is how we're starting our evening?"

"I need you to be in the mood when we get back to the room."

"Baby, with you on my mind I'm always in the mood."

"Well, I need your dick at full attention when we get back, no disruptions, just you and I enjoying every inch of one another, possibly in every inch of our room."

"Say less."

"Now, please manage to keep your eyes open so we can get to the hotel in one piece," I told him before going back to sucking his dick.

Once we got to the room, we came out of our clothes in less than two minutes. We made sure our room door was locked so Dylan's sister Destinee nor the children would interrupt us. We popped one of the pornos in and were all over one another very shortly after. This vacation served as a vacation for the children as well as a honeymoon for Dylan and I.

Dylan put the anal lube on my asshole and then slowly entered me, and I won't lie, it was a little uncomfortable at first, but only because I wasn't used to it, but once we both found our rhythm, I was good to go.

As Dylan was fucking me in the ass, he was also fingering my pussy and rubbing my clit, I think my eyes rolled into the back of my head at least a good ten times.

"Ooh, someone likes the way I'm making them feel, don't they?"

"I don't know what I'm enjoying the most, the anal sex or you fingering me and rubbing my clit at the same time," I managed to say before I began squirting all over him.

"Ooohh, I think I've unlocked a new level in Mrs. Bria Hollis, you have never squirted when we made love."

"I know, you're making me feel good all over."

"It's my job, and I take my job very seriously."

"Oh my gawd! I see!" I said as another orgasm ripped through my body.

After an hour and a half of Dylan being in damn near every hole I owned, we both climaxed together, then jumped in the shower before retiring for the night.

The next morning we were awakened to the children knocking on our room door.

"Hey my loves! Are you guys enjoying your time with your aunt Destinee?"

"Yes! She's a lot of fun, she said she can take us to the museum today so you and daddy Dylan can rest."

"Do you want us to come with y'all or would you rather go with aunt Destinee?"

"We would rather go with aunt Destinee, does that make you sad?" Paige asked.

"No it doesn't make us sad, we want you to have fun while on your vacation, so if going with aunt Destinee makes you happy, then daddy Dylan and I are happy."

"Good! We're going to breakfast then going to the museum, so we will see the both of you later."

"Tell your aunt Destinee to come here before y'all leave so we can give her money for your outing today."

"Okay mommy."

Destinee came in, we gave her about $400 for their day out today, I know how expensive my children can be, and I was pretty sure that they were going to want souvenirs from the museum, plus eat lunch while they were out, so we wanted to make sure she was covered. As soon as they left, I started the shower.

"You tryin' to take a shower without me?"

"I thought you were still asleep, I wanted to shower before going to grab breakfast real quick."

"The kids are going to breakfast too? Or did they eat already?"

"They're down there but your sister is taking them to the Children's Museum of Atlanta today, so we get to enjoy one another's company cause they don't want us tagging along."

Dylan began laughing then said, "Oh really, well, I'm not mad that I get you all to myself today."

"So am I, now let's shower so we can grab breakfast before they break everything down."

Just as I stepped in the shower, I began to feel sharp pains in my lower stomach, so I yelled out for Dylan.

"Dylan!! Dylan!!"

"Bria! What's wrong?"

"Look at the shower floor," I told him crying.

"FUCK!"

I was cramping and bleeding profusely. I'd experienced this before, I was having a miscarriage.

He helped me get dressed, then got himself dressed and we made our way to Wellstar Cobb Hospital, which was only a five minute drive from our hotel.

When we made it to the hospital, Dylan got a wheelchair so he could wheel me in. I was still bleeding heavily, but thankfully the towels I put on me were helping so I didn't bleed through my clothes. He got me checked in and the staff rushed me up to labor and delivery.

The obstetrician on duty came to see us as soon as I got into my room on the labor and delivery floor.

"Hello Mr. & Mrs. Hollis, I see here in your chart that you're pregnant and you've been bleeding for the betterment of the past thirty minutes or so, is that correct?"

"Yes, we just got to town yesterday and as I was showering this morning I felt sharp pains in my lower abdomen and then began bleeding."

"Have you been under an abnormal amount of stress lately? Lifting heavy objects?"

"No to both of your questions."
"Have you had miscarriages before?"

"Yes, I had one not too long before I got pregnant with my daughter, she's my rainbow baby."

"Ok, I'm going to do an ultrasound to see what's going on and we'll go from there."

I lifted my gown just a little so the doctor could perform the ultrasound. As the doctor was moving the probe around trying to locate the baby's heartbeat, I began to cry.

"Positive thoughts Bria, we got this," Dylan said.

"I've been through this before, we lost this baby. I'm so sorry Dylan."

The doctor finished with the ultrasound and the look on his face told us everything we needed to know, we lost the baby.

"Mr. & Mrs. Hollis, I'm sorry to tell you, but there was no fetal heartbeat."

I was numb, I knew as soon as I began to bleed what was happening, I felt worse for Dylan because this was going to be our first child together.

"We're going to perform what is called a dilation and curettage, also known as a D&C, which will clear your uterine lining to finalize the miscarriage. We will have to put you under anesthesia, I'm going to have the nurse come in with the consent forms for you to sign, then we'll get this underway and depending on how you feel afterwards, we will either keep you here for a few hours or we will discharge you to your hotel."

"Thanks doc," Dylan said tearfully.

A Month Later

"Babe, I've been thinking a lot since our miscarriage last month and I'm ready to try again for another baby, if that's something you think you're ready for."

"I'm ready but I want to make sure you're ready not only physically but mentally and emotionally as well."

"I'm good, I've been seeing a therapist and praying about it, I'm more confident now and I'm ready."

"Say no more, we can get started now if you'd like since the kids are at school."

"Say less baby," I told him, taking my robe off revealing the lingerie I had on. As soon as he saw what I had on, his dick sprang straight up.

"Someone likes what they see."

"I love everything about you my love, and when I say everything, I do mean everything," he said, grabbing me by my waist.

We hadn't made love in any capacity since the miscarriage which had been hard for the both of us because we were used to being intimate, even if it was just a quickie. I laid on the bed and Dylan just stared at me, and a small part of me was beginning to be a little self conscious.

"You are so damn beautiful, do you know that?"

"I'm glad you still think so, because I do have my moments when I feel like I'm not beautiful or when I feel as if since the miscarriage, you may be desiring someone else."

"Baby you are and will always be the only one for me, you're the only one who gets on my nerves but still makes my dick jump. The strength you showed during the miscarriage and even afterwards, made me fall in love with you all over again, you won't ever have to worry about me ever thinking or looking at another woman, my eyes, heart and body are yours, you have my word on that."

I began to cry, this man had a way with words and he wasn't the type of man to say something to try to persuade you one way or another, he definitely meant what he said and said what he meant."

I got on my knees and kissed him, the sight, smell, and taste of him, along with his patience with me during this last month made my pussy wet. I grabbed my phone and put our love making playlist on, this session was going to be special. The first song that came on was 'Get Up On It' by Kut Klose.

"Lay back so I can taste you," he told me in this sexy ass raspy voice; I obliged without hesitation.

After he ate me out I wanted to return the favor, but he declined, he said this session right here was all about me, so I didn't argue, I was just happy that we had an opportunity to enjoy one another intimately.

"Bria, let me know if anything I do hurts or is uncomfortable, I'm going to go slow."

"You know I will."

When he entered me, it was like our first time all over again, he felt heavenly dwelling inside of me. Each stroke of his was slow and sensual, he was serving me that r&b dick, his thrusts were in sync with whatever song was playing at the time. We climaxed together half an hour later, and at that very moment that his man potion filled me up, I knew he had just gotten me pregnant.

We went to shower quickly before it was time to grab the children from school.

"Babe, I know it's super early, like super, super early, but I'm pretty sure you knocked me up today."

"Oh really?"

"Yea, I don't want to jinx it though but I'm always spot on with these things."

"Well, we shall see in a few weeks," he said, kissing the back of my hand.
"Indeed we will.

Later in the year...December
A year after we met, and ten months after our tragic miscarriage, we are now a full nine months pregnant and due any day now, and I'm praying for a successful delivery and a healthy baby. We opted not to have a gender reveal because neither one of us wanted to know the gender and on the baby shower invitations, we asked our invitees to get neutral colored clothing if their gift included baby clothes.

At one o'clock in the morning on Christmas Eve, my water broke. Dylan's mother came to our place to keep an eye on the children. When we got to the hospital, I went straight up to labor and delivery, and when my midwife came in to check me, surprising enough, I was already seven centimeters dilated.

"Bria, you're more than halfway dilated, so if you keep dilating at this rate, your baby will be here within the next two hours or so."

"Damn, that's quick," Dylan said. "Being as though she has been through this twice already, with each pregnancy after the first, they typically move quicker. Do we have names picked out already?"

"If it's a boy, he will be a junior, and if it's a girl, her name will be Dior; we're still working on a middle name if the baby is a girl."

"Beautiful, just beautiful. Are you still opposed to pain meds?"

"Hell yea, ain't no needle going in my back, I don't need any new back problem because of an epidural."

"Gotcha, well, it looks like you're handling your contractions pretty well, and I know your prior two births were both natural, so let's do it mama. I'm going to go check on my other patients, if you need anything before I get back to you, just call the nurses station and I'll be right in. Do either of you need anything before I leave?"

"Nah, I think we're good, thank you," Dylan responded.

Twenty minutes and three pushes later, we were pleasantly surprised with the birth of our twins, Dylan Lamar Hollis Jr. and Dior Lyric Hollis.

"Doc, how were the twins not detected during any of the ultrasounds?" Dylan asked.

"Sometimes with twins, one twin will hide behind the other so when we do the ultrasound, we only see one fetus and hear one heartbeat, and clearly, your twins were playing hide and seek with all of us. Congratulations on the birth of your beautiful babies, you will be moved to the maternity unit soon, and mom, if you're feeling well enough and comfortable enough, you can go home tomorrow, we know the last place families want to spend Christmas in is the hospital."

"Sounds good to me, thank you for everything doc, we greatly appreciate you." "Babe, I'm going to run out, I need to get another car seat so we can get the prince and princess home safely tomorrow. Do you want me to get you something to eat before I come back?"

"You know I do, you know I don't eat this hospital food, how long do you think you're going to be?"

"Not too long, I ordered the car seat online already, so it's just a matter of picking it up. I know the stores are packed and I'm not in the mood to deal with the crowd, so ideally I should be back within the next hour."

"Great, I've been craving a burrito, so if it's not too much to ask, can you get me one please with a snapple iced tea. Please and thank you."

"You can never ask me for too much, I told you, I got you until the wheels fall off."

"Thank you my love."

I couldn't believe I was now a mother of four, if someone would have told me a year and a half ago that I'd be engaged, married and pregnant all in a span of three months, I would have told them they were lying. Dylan has made my life so much better in such a short amount of time, he is truly the man of my dreams.

My doctor discharged me a few hours after I gave birth, I was up and walking with no issues, and the babies were both of a great weight, so she saw no reason to keep me overnight. I sent a text to Dylan to tell him to pick up the other car seat from the house because I was being discharged.

When we got to the house, my mother-in-law, both of my sisters-in-law and my children had decorated the house, they even had ornaments made for the twins first Christmas, it instantly brought tears to my eyes.

"Bria, I feel like now is the most appropriate time to give you an early Christmas gift," Dylan said.

"You know you didn't have to get me anything, you've done so much already."

"Well, we can call this the icing on the cake, I know a year ago today we got engaged, and I know that our one year wedding anniversary is just a week away, so to celebrate, I got you these," he said, pulling out a set of keys and giving them to me.

"Dylan, I already have keys to our house, what are you doing?"
"You have keys to our new rental property, but those keys are the keys to our new house in Georgia, so happy anniversary and merry Christmas baby!"

I started ugly crying! The very thing that almost broke us up a year ago was what he was surprising me with, this man was full of surprises! "Baby, thank you so much, you don't know what this means to me," I told him while wiping tears from my eyes.

"I know how much this means to you, and I also know that with the business you're in and the empire you're building, Georgia is where you need to be, and wherever you are is where I am going to be. I've said it before and I'll say it again, I got you and our family until the wheels fall off or until you get tired of me, whichever comes first."

"Well you know damn well I'm never going to get tired of you, you're stuck with me in this life and in the next, I love you so much Mr. Hollis," I told him before kissing him.

"I love you too Mrs. Hollis."

"Can all of us open one gift today?" Paige asked.

"You absolutely can, pick one gift from under the tree with your name on it and have at it."

Both of the kids ran to the tree to grab one gift, my son opened a new pair of sneakers that he'd been asking us for, for a while, and my daughter opened up one of her biggest gifts, which was a student cosmetology kit since she's been saying for the longest that she wants to be a cosmetologist and makeup artist.

"Babe, I got you something as well, that will serve as both a Christmas and anniversary gift, but it won't be here until the day of our anniversary, but I'm pretty certain you're going to love it."

"Babe, you already gave me the best Christmas and anniversary when you blessed me with not one baby but two today. I also have another surprise for you and the children, but I will give that to y'all tomorrow."

A Week Later

It was a little past ten in the morning on the day of my and Dylan's one year wedding anniversary, and there was a knock on our door.

"Babe, can you get the door please?" I knew it was his gift from me so I wanted him to be the one to answer the door.

"Yea, are you expecting company?"

"Nope."

After I heard the door close, he came running into the bedroom.

"Babe, I know you didn't do what you think you did," he said, holding up the keys to his new Ford Expedition.

"I know you've been eyeing suv's and because of our growing family, I knew at least one of us needed a larger vehicle, so I figured it should be you."

"You are so selfless and giving, I'm not sure what I did to deserve you, but I'm so happy you are my partner in life and for life."

"As much as you do for our family, you deserved it baby, I love you, the children love you and we all appreciate you, so that is a small token of our appreciation," I told him before kissing him.

We decided to celebrate our anniversary as a family, so we all went out to eat later that evening. Dylan wanted to christen the new truck but I told him to give me at least another week and then we could christen every inch of that truck. Now don't judge me cause it hasn't been six weeks, but baby, quiet as it's kept, I've been wanting to feel my man inside of me since the night I gave birth. Knowing this would be our last holiday spent in Connecticut was bittersweet but I for one was ready to start our new chapter in Georgia.

I hope you find your forever love like I found mine and I pray they treat you as well as my man treats me. For someone who used to not like the holiday season, I guess it's safe to say Dylan has made me love the holiday season now. This is now the end of our love story! At least for now. Smooches!

Made in the USA
Middletown, DE
13 December 2025

23231949R00154